Romeo and Juliet

William Shakespeare

(Annotated)

Copyright

Author: William Shakespeare

Editor:The Secret Bookshelf

Contributor:John W. cousin

Contents

The Author

Shakespeare, William (1564–1616). — Dramatist and poet, born at Stratford-on-Avon, Warwickshire, on 22nd or 23rd, and baptised on 26th April, 1564. On his father's side he belonged to a good yeoman stock, though his descent cannot be certainly traced beyond his grandfather, a Richard S., settled at Snitterfield, near Stratford. His father, John S., appears to have been a man of intelligence and energy, who set up in Stratford as a dealer in all kinds of agricultural produce, to which he added the trade of a glover. He became prosperous, and gained the respect of his neighbours, as is evidenced by his election in succession to all the municipal honours of his community, including those of chief alderman and high bailiff. He married Mary, youngest daughter of Robert Arden, a wealthy farmer at Wilmcote, and a younger branch of a family of considerable distinction, and whose tenant Richard S.

had been. On her father's death Mary inherited Asbies, a house with 50 acres of land attached to it. The first children of the marriage were two daughter, who died in infancy. William was the third, and others followed, of whom three sons, Gilbert, Richard, and Edmund, and a daughter Joan, reached maturity. He was *ed.* with his brother Gilbert at Stratford Grammar School, where he learned Latin from Lilly's Grammar, English, writing, and arithmetic. He probably read some of the Latin classics and may have got a little Greek, and though his learned friend Ben Jonson credits him with "little Latin and less Greek," Aubrey says he "knew Latin pretty well." This happy state of matters continued until he was about 13, when his father fell into misfortune, which appears to have gone on deepening until the success and prosperity of the poet in later years enabled him to reinstate the family in its former position. Meanwhile, however, he was taken from school, and appears to have been made to assist his father in his business. The next certain fact in his history is his marriage in November, 1582, when he was 18, to Ann Hathaway, daughter of a yeoman at the neighbouring hamlet of Shottery, and 8 years his senior. Various circumstances point to the marriage having been against the wishes of his own family, and pressed on by that of his wife, and that it was so urged in defence of the reputation of the lady, and as perhaps might be expected, they indicate, though not conclusively, that it did not prove altogether happy. The birth, in May, 1583, of his eldest child Susannah (who is said to have inherited something of his wit and practical ability, and who married a Dr. John Hall), followed in the next year by that of twins, Hamnet and Judith, and the necessity of increased means, led to his departure from Stratford, whence he travelled on foot to London, where the next 23 years of his life were mainly spent. The tradition that his departure was also caused by trouble into which he had got by killing the deer of Sir Thomas Lucy, of

Charlcote, is credible. Leaving Stratford in 1585 or the beginning of 1586, he seems at once to have turned to the theatres, where he soon found work, although, as Rowe, his first biographer, says, "in a very mean rank." It was not long, however, before he had opportunities of showing his capacities as an actor, with the result that he shortly became a member of one of the chief acting companies of the day, which was then under the patronage of the Earl of Leicester, and after being associated with the names of various other noblemen, at last on the accession of James I. became known as the King's Company. It played originally in "The Theatre" in Shoreditch, the first playhouse to be erected in England, and afterwards in the "Rose" on the Bankside, Southwark, the scene of the earliest successes of S. as an actor and playwright. Subsequently to 1594, he acted occasionally in a playhouse in Newington Butts, and between 1595 and 1599 in the "Curtain." In the latter year the "Globe" was built on the Bankside, and 10 years later the "Blackfriars:" and with these two, but especially with the former, the remainder of his professional life was associated. It is not unlikely that he visited various provincial towns; but that he was ever in Scotland or on the Continent is improbable. Among the plays in which he appeared were Jonson's Every Man in his Humour and Sejanus, and in Hamlet he played "The Ghost;" and it is said that his brother Gilbert as an old man remembered his appearing as "Adam" in As You Like It. By 1595 S. was famous and prosperous; his earlier plays had been written and acted, and his poems Venus and Adonis, and Lucrece, and probably most of the sonnets, had been published and received with extraordinary favour. He had also powerful friends and patrons, including the Earl of Southampton, and was known at Court. By the end of the century he is mentioned by Francis Meres (q.v.) as the greatest man of letters of the day, and his name had become so valuable that it was affixed by unscrupulous publishers to works, e.g. Locrine, Oldcastle, and The Yorkshire Tragedy, by other and often very inferior hands. He had also resumed a close connection with Stratford, and was making the restoration of the family position there the object of his ambition. In accordance with this he induced his father to apply for a grant of arms, which was given, and he purchased New Place, the largest house in the village. With the income derived from his profession as an actor and dramatist, and his share of the profits of the Globe and Blackfriars theatres, and in view of the business capacity with which he managed his affairs, he may be regarded as almost a wealthy man, and he went on adding to his influence in Stratford by buying land. He had enjoyed the favour of Elizabeth, and her death in 1603 did nothing to disturb his fortunes, as he stood quite as well with her successor. His company received the title of the "King's Servants," and his plays were frequently performed before the Court. But notwithstanding this, the clouds had gathered over his life. The conspiracy of Essex in 1601 had involved several of his friends and patrons in disaster; he had himself been entangled in the unhappy love affair which is supposed to be referred to in some of his sonnets, and he had suffered unkindness at the hands of a friend. For a few years his dramas breathe the darkness and bitterness of a heart which has been sounding the depths of sad experience. He soon, however, emerged from this and, passing through the period of the great tragedies, reached the serene triumph and peace of his later dramas. In 1611 S. severed his long connection with the stage, and retired to Stratford, where the remaining five years of his life were spent in honour and prosperity. Early in 1616 his health began to give way, and he made his will. In the spring he received a visit from his friends, Jonson and Drayton, and the festivity with which it was celebrated seems to have brought on a fever, of which he died on April 23. He was survived by his wife and his two daughter, both of whom were married. His descendants died out with his grand-daughter, Elizabeth Hall.

Immense research has been spent upon the writings of S., with the result of substantial agreement as to the order of their production and the sources from which their subjects were drawn; for S. rarely troubled himself with the construction of a story, but adopting one already existing reared upon it as a foundation one of those marvellous superstructures which make him the greatest painter and interpreter of human character the world has ever seen. His period of literary production extends from about 1588 to 1613, and falls naturally into four divisions, which Prof. Dowden has named, "In the Workshop" ending in 1596; "In the World" 1596–1601; "Out of the Depths" 1601–1608; and "On the Heights" 1608–1613. Of the 37 plays usually attributed to him, 16 only were published during his lifetime, so that the exact order in which they were produced cannot always be determined with certainty. Recent authorities are agreed to the extent that while they do not invariably place the individual plays in the same order, they are almost entirely at one as to which belong to the four periods respectively. The following list shows in a condensed form the order according to Mr. Sidney Lee (Dictionary of National Biography) with the most probable dates and the original sources on which the plays are founded.

Chronological Table of Shakespeare's Plays

First Period — 1588?-1596

LOVE'S LABOUR LOST (1591) — Plot probably original.

TWO GENTLEMEN OF VERONA (1591) — *The Shepherdess Felismena* in George of Montmayor's *Diana*.

COMEDY OF ERRORS (1591) — *Menæchmi* of Plautus and earlier play.

ROMEO AND JULIET (1591) — Italian romance in

Painter's *Palace of Pleasure* and Broke's *Romeus and Juliet*.

HENRY VI. 1, 2, and 3 (1592) — Retouched old plays, probably with Marlowe.

RICHARD III. (1592–3) — Holinshed's *Chronicle*.

RICHARD II. (1593–4?) — do.

TITUS ANDRONICUS (1594) — Probably chiefly by Kyd, retouched.

KING JOHN (1594) — Old play retouched.

Second Period — 1596–1601-2

MERCHANT OF VENICE (1594) — Italian novels, *Gesta Romanorum*, and earlier plays.

MIDSUMMER NIGHT'S DREAM (1595) — North's *Plutarch*, Chaucer, Ovid.

ALL'S WELL THAT ENDS WELL (1595) — Painter's *Palace of Pleasure*.

TAMING OF THE SHREW (1596?) — Old play retouched, and *Supposes* of G. Gascoigne, Shakespeare's in part only.

HENRY IV. 1 and 2 (1597?) — Holinshed and earlier play.

MERRY WIVES OF WINDSOR (1597–8) — Italian novels (?).

HENRY V. (1599).

MUCH ADO ABOUT NOTHING (1599) — Partly from Italian.

AS YOU LIKE IT (1599) — Lodge's *Rosalynde, Euphues' Golden Legacie.*

TWELFTH NIGHT (1599) — B. Riche's *Apolonius and Silla.*

Third Period — 1602–1608

JULIUS CÆSAR (1601) — North's *Plutarch.*

HAMLET (1601–2) — Belleforest's *Histoires Tragiques.*

TROILUS AND CRESSIDA (1603?) — Probably Chaucer's *Troilus and Cresseide* and Chapman's *Homer.*

OTHELLO (1604) — Cinthio's *Hecatommithi.*

MEASURE FOR MEASURE (1604?) — Cinthio's

Epithia.

MACBETH (1605–6?) — Holinshed.

LEAR (1606) — do.

TIMON OF ATHENS (1607?) — *Palace of Pleasure*

and Plutarch written with G. Wilkins (?) and W.

Rowley (?).

PERICLES (1607–8) — Gower's *Confessio Amantis,*

with G. Wilkins (?).

ANTONY AND CLEOPATRA (1608) — North's

Plutarch.

CORIOLANUS (1608) — do.

Fourth Period — 1608–1613

CYMBELINE (1610–11?) — Holinshed and *Ginevra*

in Boccaccio's *Decamerone.*

WINTER'S TALE (1610–11) — Green's *Dorastus*

and Fawnia.

TEMPEST (1611?) — S. Jourdain's *Discovery of the*

Bermudas.

HENRY VIII. (1612–13) — Draft by S. completed by Fletcher and perhaps Massinger.

Poems

VENUS AND ADONIS (1593).

RAPE OF LUCRECE (1594).

SONNETS (1591–94?).

The evidence as to chronology is three-fold — (1) External, such as entries in registers of Stationers' Company, contemporary references, or details as to the companies of actors; (2) External and internal combined, such as references in the plays to events or books, etc.; (3) Internal, content and treatment, progressive changes in versification, presence of frequency of rhyme, etc. The genius of S. was so intensely dramatic that it is impossible to say confidently when he speaks in his own character. The sonnets, written probably 1591–94 have, however, been thought to be of a more personal nature, and to contain indications as to his character and history, and much labour and ingenuity have been expended to make them yield their secrets. It is generally agreed that they fall into two sections, the first consisting of sonnets 1 to 126 addressed to a young man, probably Henry Wriothesley, Earl of Southampton, the friend and patron of S., and 9 years his junior; and the second from 127 to 154 addressed or referring to a woman in whose snares the writer had become entangled, and by whom he was betrayed. Some, however, have held that they are allegorical, or partly written on behalf of others, or that the emotion they express is dramatic and not personal.

There are contemporary references to S. which show him to have been generally held in high regard. Thus Ben Jonson says, "I loved the man, and do honour to his memory, on this side idolatry, as much as any," and Chettle refers to "His demeanour no lesse civil than exelent in the qualities he professes." The only exception is a reference to him in Greene's Groat's-worth of Wit, as "an upstart crow beautified with our feathers, that with his tyger's heart wrapt in a player's hide supposes he is as well able to bumbast out a blanke verse as the best of you . . . and is in his own conceit the only Shake-scene in a countrie." He is said to have written rapidly and with facility, rarely requiring to alter what he had set down. In addition to his generally received works, others have been attributed to him, some of which have been already mentioned: the only two which appear to have serious claims to consideration are *The Two Noble Kinsmen*, partly by Fletcher, and *Edward III.*, of which part of Act I. and the whole of Act II. have been thought to be Shakespeare's. On the other hand a theory has been propounded that none of the plays bearing his name were really his, but that they were written by Bacon (*q.v.*). This extraordinary view has been widely supported, chiefly in America, and has been sometimes maintained; with considerable ability and misplaced ingenuity.

Summary. — Born 1564, *ed.* at Stratford School, father falls into difficulties *c.* 1577, married Ann Hathaway 1582, goes to London end of 1585, finds employment in theatres and acts in chief companies of the time, first in "The Theatre" afterwards the "Rose," the "Curtain," the "Globe" and "Blackfriars," appearing in Jonson's *Every Man in his Humour* and *Sejanus*. *Venus and Adonis, Lucrece,* earlier plays, and perhaps most of sonnets published by 1595, when he was friend of Southampton and known at Court, purchases New Place at Stratford, falls into trouble *c.* 1600, having lost friends in Essex's conspiracy, and has unfortunate love affair; emerges from this into honour and peace, retires to Stratford and died 1616. Productive period *c.* 1588–1613, 4 divisions, first (1588–96), second (1596–1601), third (1601–1608), fourth (1608–1613). Of 37 plays usually attributed, only 16 published in his life.

As might have been expected, there is a copious literature devoted to Shakespeare and his works. Among those dealing with biography may be mentioned Halliwell Phillipps's *Outline of the Life of Shakespeare* (7th ed., 1887), Fleay's *Shakespeare Manual* (1876), and *Life of Shakespeare* (1886). *Life* by S. Lee (1898), Dowden's *Shakespeare, his Mind and Art* (1875), Drake's *Shakespeare and his Times* (1817), Thornberry's *Shakespeare's England* (1856), Knight's *Shakespeare* (1843). *See* also Works by Guizot, De Quincey, Fullom, Elze, and others. Criticisms by Coleridge, Hazlitt, Swinburne, T.S. Baynes, and others. Concordance by Mrs. Cowden Clarke. Ed., Rowe (1709), Pope (1725), Theobald (1733), Johnson (1765), Capell (1768), Steevens's improved re-issue of Johnson (1773), Malone (1790), Reed's *1st Variorum* (1803), *2nd Variorum* (1813),

3rd Variorum by Jas. Boswell the younger (1821), Dyce (1857), Staunton (1868–70), Cambridge by W.G. Clark and Dr. Aldis Wright (1863–66), Temple (ed. I. Gollancz, 1894–96), *Eversley Shakespeare* (ed. Herford, 1899)

Persons Represented

Escalus, Prince of Verona. Paris, a young Nobleman, kinsman to the Prince. Montague,}Heads of two Houses at variance with each other. Capulet, } An Old Man, Uncle to Capulet. Romeo, Son to Montague. Mercutio, Kinsman to the Prince, and Friend to Romeo. Benvolio, Nephew to Montague, and Friend to Romeo. Tybalt, Nephew to Lady Capulet. Friar Lawrence, a Franciscan. Friar John, of the same Order. Balthasar, Servant to Romeo. Sampson, Servant to Capulet. Gregory, Servant to Capulet. Peter, Servant to Juliet's Nurse. Abraham, Servant to Montague. An Apothecary. Three Musicians. Chorus. Page to Paris; another Page. An Officer.

Lady Montague, Wife to Montague. Lady Capulet, Wife to Capulet. Juliet, Daughter to Capulet. Nurse to Juliet.

Citizens of Verona; several Men and Women, relations to both houses; Maskers, Guards, Watchmen, and Attendants.

Scene-During the Greater Part of the Play In Verona; Once, In the Fifth Act, At Mantua.

The Prologue

[Enter Chorus.]

Chor. Two households, both alike in dignity, In fair Verona, where we lay our scene, From ancient grudge break to new mutiny, Where civil blood makes civil hands unclean. From forth the fatal loins of these two foes A pair of star-cross'd lovers take their life; Whose misadventur'd piteous overthrows Doth with their death bury their parents' strife. The fearful passage of their death-mark'd love, And the continuance of their parents' rage, Which but their children's end naught could remove, Is now the two hours' traffic of our stage; The which, if you with patient ears attend, What here shall miss, our toil shall strive to mend.

Act I

Scene I. A Public Place.

[Enter Sampson and Gregory armed with swords and bucklers.]

Sampson. Gregory, o' my word, we'll not carry coals.

Gregory. No, for then we should be colliers.

Sampson. I mean, an we be in choler we'll draw.

Gregory. Ay, while you live, draw your neck out o' the collar.

Sampson. I strike quickly, being moved.

Gregory. But thou art not quickly moved to strike.

Sampson. A dog of the house of Montague moves me.

Gregory. To move is to stir; and to be valiant is to stand: therefore, if thou art moved, thou runn'st away.

Sampson. A dog of that house shall move me to stand: I will take the wall of any man or maid of Montague's.

Gregory. That shows thee a weak slave; for the weakest goes to the wall.

Sampson. True; and therefore women, being the weaker vessels, are ever thrust to the wall: therefore I will push Montague's men from the wall and thrust his maids to the wall.

Gregory. The quarrel is between our masters and us their men.

Sampson. 'Tis all one, I will show myself a tyrant: when I have fought with the men I will be cruel with the maids, I will cut off their heads.

Gregory. The heads of the maids?

Sampson. Ay, the heads of the maids, or their maidenheads; take it in what sense thou wilt.

Gregory. They must take it in sense that feel it.

Sampson. Me they shall feel while I am able to stand: and 'tis known I am a pretty piece of flesh.

Gregory. 'Tis well thou art not fish; if thou hadst, thou hadst been poor-John.--Draw thy tool; Here comes two of the house of Montagues.

Sampson. My naked weapon is out: quarrel! I will back thee.

Gregory. How! turn thy back and run?

Sampson. Fear me not.

Gregory. No, marry; I fear thee!

Sampson. Let us take the law of our sides; let them begin.

Gregory. I will frown as I pass by; and let them take it as they list.

Sampson. Nay, as they dare. I will bite my thumb at them; which is disgrace to them if they bear it.

[Enter Abraham and Balthasar.]

Abraham. Do you bite your thumb at us, sir?

Sampson. I do bite my thumb, sir.

Abraham. Do you bite your thumb at us, sir?

Sampson. Is the law of our side if I say ay?

Gregory. No.

Sampson. No, sir, I do not bite my thumb at you, sir; but I bite my thumb, sir.

Gregory. Do you quarrel, sir?

Abraham. Quarrel, sir! no, sir.

Sampson. But if you do, sir, am for you: I serve as good a man as you.

Abraham. No better.

Sampson. Well, sir.

Gregory. Say better; here comes one of my master's kinsmen.

Sampson. Yes, better, sir.

Abraham. You lie.

Sampson. Draw, if you be men.--Gregory, remember thy swashing blow.

[They fight.]

[Enter Benvolio.]

Benvolio. Part, fools! put up your swords; you know not what you do. [Beats down their swords.]

[Enter Tybalt.]

Tybalt. What, art thou drawn among these heartless hinds? Turn thee Benvolio, look upon thy death.

Benvolio. I do but keep the peace: put up thy sword, Or manage it to part these men with me.

Tybalt. What, drawn, and talk of peace! I hate the word As I hate hell, all Montagues, and thee: Have at thee, coward!

[They fight.]

[Enter several of both Houses, who join the fray; then enter Citizens with clubs.]

1 Citizen. Clubs, bills, and partisans! strike! beat them down! Down with the Capulets! Down with the Montagues!

[Enter Capulet in his gown, and Lady Capulet.]

Capulet. What noise is this?--Give me my long sword, ho!

Lady Capulet. A crutch, a crutch!--Why call you for a sword?

Capulet. My sword, I say!--Old Montague is come, And flourishes his blade in spite of me.

[Enter Montague and his Lady Montague.]

Montague. Thou villain Capulet!-- Hold me not, let me go.

Lady Montague. Thou shalt not stir one foot to seek a foe.

[Enter Prince, with Attendants.]

Prince. Rebellious subjects, enemies to peace, Profaners of this neighbour-stained steel,-- Will they not hear?--What, ho! you men, you beasts, That quench the fire of your pernicious rage With purple fountains issuing from your veins,-- On pain of torture, from those bloody hands Throw your mistemper'd weapons to the ground And hear the sentence of your moved prince.-- Three civil brawls, bred of an airy word, By thee, old Capulet, and Montague, Have thrice disturb'd the quiet of our streets; And made Verona's ancient citizens Cast by their grave beseeming ornaments, To wield old partisans, in hands as old, Canker'd with peace, to part your canker'd hate: If ever you disturb our streets again, Your lives shall pay the forfeit of the peace. For this time, all the rest depart away:-- You, Capulet, shall go along with me;-- And, Montague, come you this afternoon, To know our farther pleasure in this case, To old Free-town, our common judgment-place.-- Once more, on pain of death, all men depart.

[Exeunt Prince and Attendants; Capulet, Lady Capulet, Tybalt, Citizens, and Servants.]

Montague. Who set this ancient quarrel new abroach?-- Speak, nephew, were you by when it began?

Benvolio. Here were the servants of your adversary And yours, close fighting ere I did approach: I drew to part them: in the instant came The fiery Tybalt, with his sword prepar'd; Which, as he breath'd defiance to my ears, He swung about his head, and cut the winds, Who, nothing hurt withal, hiss'd him in scorn: While we were interchanging thrusts and blows, Came more and more, and fought on part and part, Till the prince came, who parted either part.

Lady Montague. O, where is Romeo?--saw you him to-day?-- Right glad I am he was not at this fray.

Benvolio. Madam, an hour before the worshipp'd sun Peer'd forth the golden window of the east, A troubled mind drave me to walk abroad; Where,--underneath the grove of sycamore That westward rooteth from the city's side,-- So early walking did I see your son: Towards him I made; but he was ware of me, And stole into the covert of the wood: I, measuring his affections by my own,-- That most are busied when they're most alone,-- Pursu'd my humour, not pursuing his, And gladly shunn'd who gladly fled from me.

Montague. Many a morning hath he there been seen, With tears augmenting the fresh morning's dew, Adding to clouds more clouds with his deep sighs: But all so soon as the all-cheering sun Should in the farthest east begin to draw The shady curtains from Aurora's bed, Away from light steals home my heavy son, And private in his chamber pens himself; Shuts up his windows, locks fair daylight out And makes himself an artificial night: Black and portentous must this humour prove, Unless good counsel may the cause remove.

Benvolio. My noble uncle, do you know the cause?

Montague. I neither know it nor can learn of him.

Benvolio. Have you importun'd him by any means?

Montague. Both by myself and many other friends; But he, his own affections' counsellor, Is to himself,--I will not say how true,-- But to himself so secret and so close, So far from sounding and discovery, As is the bud bit with an envious worm Ere he can spread his sweet leaves to the air, Or dedicate his beauty to the sun. Could we but learn from whence his sorrows grow, We would as willingly give cure as know.

Benvolio. See, where he comes: so please you step aside; I'll know his grievance or be much denied.

Montague. I would thou wert so happy by thy stay To hear true shrift.--Come, madam, let's away,

[Exeunt Montague and Lady.]

[Enter Romeo.]

Benvolio. Good morrow, cousin.

Romeo. Is the day so young?

Benvolio. But new struck nine.

Romeo. Ay me! sad hours seem long. Was that my father that went hence so fast?

Benvolio. It was.--What sadness lengthens Romeo's hours?

Romeo. Not having that which, having, makes them short.

Benvolio. In love?

Romeo. Out,-

Benvolio. Of love?

Romeo. Out of her favour where I am in love.

Benvolio. Alas, that love, so gentle in his view, Should be so tyrannous and rough in proof!

Romeo. Alas that love, whose view is muffled still, Should, without eyes, see pathways to his will!-- Where shall we dine?--O me!--What fray was here? Yet tell me not, for I have heard it all. Here's much to do with hate, but more with love:-- Why, then, O brawling love! O loving hate! O anything, of nothing first create! O heavy lightness! serious vanity! Mis-shapen chaos of well-seeming forms! Feather of lead, bright smoke, cold fire, sick health! Still-waking sleep, that is not what it is!-- This love feel I, that feel no love in this. Dost thou not laugh?

Benvolio. No, coz, I rather weep.

Romeo. Good heart, at what?

Benvolio. At thy good heart's oppression.

Romeo. Why, such is love's transgression.-- Griefs of mine own lie heavy in my breast; Which thou wilt propagate, to have it prest With more of thine: this love that thou hast shown Doth add more grief to too much of mine own. Love is a smoke rais'd with the fume of sighs; Being purg'd, a fire sparkling in lovers' eyes; Being vex'd, a sea nourish'd with lovers' tears: What is it else? a madness most discreet, A choking gall, and a preserving sweet.- Farewell, my coz.

[Going.]

Benvolio. Soft! I will go along: An if you leave me so, you do me wrong.

Romeo. Tut! I have lost myself; I am not here: This is not Romeo, he's some other where.

Benvolio. Tell me in sadness who is that you love?

Romeo. What, shall I groan and tell thee?

Benvolio. Groan! why, no; But sadly tell me who.

Romeo. Bid a sick man in sadness make his will,-- Ah, word ill urg'd to one that is so ill!-- In sadness, cousin, I do love a woman.

Benvolio. I aim'd so near when I suppos'd you lov'd.

Romeo. A right good markman!--And she's fair I love.

Benvolio. A right fair mark, fair coz, is soonest hit.

Romeo. Well, in that hit you miss: she'll not be hit With Cupid's arrow,--she hath Dian's wit; And, in strong proof of chastity well arm'd, From love's weak childish bow she lives unharm'd. She will not stay the siege of loving terms Nor bide th' encounter of assailing eyes, Nor ope her lap to saint-seducing gold: O, she's rich in beauty; only poor That, when she dies, with beauty dies her store.

Benvolio. Then she hath sworn that she will still live chaste?

Romeo. She hath, and in that sparing makes huge waste; For beauty, starv'd with her severity, Cuts beauty off from all posterity. She is too fair, too wise; wisely too fair, To merit bliss by making me despair: She hath forsworn to love; and in that vow Do I live dead that live to tell it now.

Benvolio. Be rul'd by me, forget to think of her.

Romeo. O, teach me how I should forget to think.

Benvolio. By giving liberty unto thine eyes; Examine other beauties.

Romeo. 'Tis the way To call hers, exquisite, in question more: These happy masks that kiss fair ladies' brows, Being black, puts us in mind they hide the fair; He that is strucken blind cannot forget The precious treasure of his eyesight lost: Show me a mistress that is

passing fair, What doth her beauty serve but as a note

Where I may read who pass'd that passing fair?

Farewell: thou canst not teach me to forget.

Benvolio. I'll pay that doctrine, or else die in debt.

[Exeunt.]

Scene II. A Street.

[Enter Capulet, Paris, and Servant.]

Capulet. But Montague is bound as well as I, In penalty alike; and 'tis not hard, I think, For men so old as we to keep the peace.

Paris. Of honourable reckoning are you both; And pity 'tis you liv'd at odds so long. But now, my lord, what say you to my suit?

Capulet. But saying o'er what I have said before: My child is yet a stranger in the world, She hath not seen the change of fourteen years; Let two more summers wither in their pride Ere we may think her ripe to be a bride.

Paris. Younger than she are happy mothers made.

Capulet. And too soon marr'd are those so early made. The earth hath swallowed all my hopes but she,-- She is the hopeful lady of my earth: But woo her, gentle Paris, get her heart, My will to her consent is but a part;

An she agree, within her scope of choice Lies my consent and fair according voice. This night I hold an old accustom'd feast, Whereto I have invited many a guest, Such as I love; and you among the store, One more, most welcome, makes my number more. At my poor house look to behold this night Earth-treading stars that make dark heaven light: Such comfort as do lusty young men feel When well apparell'd April on the heel Of limping winter treads, even such delight Among fresh female buds shall you this night Inherit at my house; hear all, all see, And like her most whose merit most shall be: Which, among view of many, mine, being one, May stand in number, though in reckoning none. Come, go with me.--Go, sirrah, trudge about Through fair Verona; find those persons out Whose names are written there, [gives a paper] and to them say, My house and welcome on their pleasure stay.

[Exeunt Capulet and Paris].

Servant.Find them out whose names are written here! It is written that the shoemaker should meddle with his yard and the tailor with his last, the fisher with his pencil, and the painter with his nets; but I am sent to find those persons whose names are here writ, and can never find what names the writing person hath here writ. I must to the learned:--in good time!

[Enter Benvolio and Romeo.]

Benvolio. Tut, man, one fire burns out another's burning, One pain is lessen'd by another's anguish; Turn giddy, and be holp by backward turning; One desperate grief cures with another's languish: Take thou some new infection to thy eye, And the rank poison of the old will die.

Romeo. Your plantain-leaf is excellent for that.

Benvolio. For what, I pray thee?

Romeo. For your broken shin.

Benvolio. Why, Romeo, art thou mad?

Romeo. Not mad, but bound more than a madman is;

Shut up in prison, kept without my food, Whipp'd and

tormented and--God-den, good fellow.

Servant. God gi' go-den.--I pray, sir, can you read?

Romeo. Ay, mine own fortune in my misery.

Servant. Perhaps you have learned it without book:

but I pray, can you read anything you see?

Romeo. Ay, If I know the letters and the language.

Servant. Ye say honestly: rest you merry!

Romeo. Stay, fellow; I can read. [Reads.] 'Signior

Martino and his wife and daughters; County Anselmo

and his beauteous sisters; the lady widow of Vitruvio;

Signior Placentio and his lovely nieces; Mercutio and

his brother Valentine; mine uncle Capulet, his wife, and

daughters; my fair niece Rosaline; Livia; Signior

Valentio and his cousin Tybalt; Lucio and the lively

Helena.' A fair assembly. [Gives back the paper]:

whither should they come?

Servant. Up.

Romeo. Whither?

Servant. To supper; to our house.

Romeo. Whose house?

Servant. My master's.

Romeo. Indeed I should have ask'd you that before.

Servant. Now I'll tell you without asking: my master is the great rich Capulet; and if you be not of the house of Montagues, I pray, come and crush a cup of wine. Rest you merry!

[Exit.]

Benvolio. At this same ancient feast of Capulet's Sups the fair Rosaline whom thou so lov'st; With all the admired beauties of Verona. Go thither; and, with unattainted eye, Compare her face with some that I shall show, And I will make thee think thy swan a crow.

Romeo. When the devout religion of mine eye Maintains such falsehood, then turn tears to fires; And these,--who, often drown'd, could never die,--

Transparent heretics, be burnt for liars! One fairer than my love? the all-seeing sun Ne'er saw her match since first the world begun.

Benvolio. Tut, you saw her fair, none else being by, Herself pois'd with herself in either eye: But in that crystal scales let there be weigh'd Your lady's love against some other maid That I will show you shining at this feast, And she shall scant show well that now shows best.

Romeo. I'll go along, no such sight to be shown, But to rejoice in splendour of my own.

[Exeunt.]

Scene III. Room in Capulet's House.

[Enter Lady Capulet, and Nurse.]

Lady Capulet. Nurse, where's my daughter? call her forth to me.

Nurse. Now, by my maidenhea,--at twelve year old,-- I bade her come.--What, lamb! what ladybird!-- God forbid!--where's this girl?--what, Juliet!

[Enter Juliet.]

Juliet. How now, who calls?

Nurse. Your mother.

Juliet. Madam, I am here. What is your will?

Lady Capulet. This is the matter,--Nurse, give leave awhile, We must talk in secret: nurse, come back again; I have remember'd me, thou's hear our counsel. Thou knowest my daughter's of a pretty age.

Nurse. Faith, I can tell her age unto an hour.

Lady Capulet. She's not fourteen.

Nurse. I'll lay fourteen of my teeth,-- And yet, to my teen be it spoken, I have but four,-- She is not fourteen. How long is it now To Lammas-tide?

Lady Capulet. A fortnight and odd days.

Nurse. Even or odd, of all days in the year, Come Lammas-eve at night shall she be fourteen. Susan and she,--God rest all Christian souls!-- Were of an age: well, Susan is with God; She was too good for me:--but, as I said, On Lammas-eve at night shall she be fourteen; That shall she, marry; I remember it well. 'Tis since the earthquake now eleven years; And she was wean'd,--I never shall forget it--, Of all the days of the year, upon that day: For I had then laid wormwood to my dug, Sitting in the sun under the dove-house wall; My lord and you were then at Mantua: Nay, I do bear a brain:-- but, as I said, When it did taste the wormwood on the nipple Of my dug and felt it bitter, pretty fool, To see it tetchy, and fall out with the dug! Shake, quoth the dove-house: 'twas no need, I trow, To bid me trudge.

And since that time it is eleven years; For then she could stand alone; nay, by the rood She could have run and waddled all about; For even the day before, she broke her brow: And then my husband,--God be with his soul! 'A was a merry man,--took up the child: 'Yea,' quoth he, 'dost thou fall upon thy face? Thou wilt fall backward when thou hast more wit; Wilt thou not, Jule?' and, by my holidame, The pretty wretch left crying, and said 'Ay:' To see now how a jest shall come about! I warrant, an I should live a thousand yeas, I never should forget it; 'Wilt thou not, Jule?' quoth he; And, pretty fool, it stinted, and said 'Ay.'

Lady Capulet. Enough of this; I pray thee hold thy peace.

Nurse. Yes, madam;--yet I cannot choose but laugh, To think it should leave crying, and say 'Ay:' And yet, I warrant, it had upon its brow A bump as big as a young cockerel's stone; A parlous knock; and it cried bitterly. 'Yea,' quoth my husband, 'fall'st upon thy face? Thou wilt fall backward when thou com'st to age; Wilt thou not, Jule?' it stinted, and said 'Ay.'

Juliet. And stint thou too, I pray thee, nurse, say I.

Nurse. Peace, I have done. God mark thee to his grace! Thou wast the prettiest babe that e'er I nurs'd: An I might live to see thee married once, I have my wish.

Lady Capulet. Marry, that marry is the very theme I came to talk of.--Tell me, daughter Juliet, How stands your disposition to be married?

Juliet. It is an honour that I dream not of.

Nurse. An honour!--were not I thine only nurse, I would say thou hadst suck'd wisdom from thy teat.

Lady Capulet. Well, think of marriage now: younger than you, Here in Verona, ladies of esteem, Are made already mothers: by my count I was your mother much upon these years That you are now a maid. Thus, then, in brief;-- The valiant Paris seeks you for his love.

Nurse. A man, young lady! lady, such a man As all the world--why he's a man of wax.

Lady Capulet. Verona's summer hath not such a flower.

Nurse. Nay, he's a flower, in faith, a very flower.

Lady Capulet. What say you? can you love the gentleman? This night you shall behold him at our feast; Read o'er the volume of young Paris' face, And find delight writ there with beauty's pen; Examine every married lineament, And see how one another lends content; And what obscur'd in this fair volume lies Find written in the margent of his eyes. This precious book of love, this unbound lover, To beautify him, only lacks a cover: The fish lives in the sea; and 'tis much pride For fair without the fair within to hide: That book in many's eyes doth share the glory, That in gold clasps locks in the golden story; So shall you share all that he doth possess, By having him, making yourself no less.

Nurse. No less! nay, bigger; women grow by men

Lady Capulet. Speak briefly, can you like of Paris' love?

Juliet. I'll look to like, if looking liking move: But no more deep will I endart mine eye Than your consent gives strength to make it fly.

[Enter a Servant.]

Servant. Madam, the guests are come, supper served up, you called, my young lady asked for, the nurse cursed in the pantry, and everything in extremity. I must hence to wait; I beseech you, follow straight.

Lady Capulet. We follow thee. [Exit Servant.]-- Juliet, the county stays.

Nurse. Go, girl, seek happy nights to happy days.

[Exeunt.]

Scene IV. A Street.

[Enter Romeo, Mercutio, Benvolio, with five or six Maskers; Torch-bearers, and others.]

Romeo. What, shall this speech be spoke for our excuse? Or shall we on without apology?

Benvolio. The date is out of such prolixity: We'll have no Cupid hoodwink'd with a scarf, Bearing a Tartar's painted bow of lath, Scaring the ladies like a crow-keeper; Nor no without-book prologue, faintly spoke After the prompter, for our entrance: But, let them measure us by what they will, We'll measure them a measure, and be gone.

Romeo. Give me a torch,--I am not for this ambling; Being but heavy, I will bear the light.

Mercutio. Nay, gentle Romeo, we must have you dance.

Romeo. Not I, believe me: you have dancing shoes, With nimble soles; I have a soul of lead So stakes me to the ground I cannot move.

Mercutio. You are a lover; borrow Cupid's wings, And soar with them above a common bound.

Romeo. I am too sore enpierced with his shaft To soar with his light feathers; and so bound, I cannot bound a pitch above dull woe: Under love's heavy burden do I sink.

Mercutio. And, to sink in it, should you burden love; Too great oppression for a tender thing.

Romeo. Is love a tender thing? it is too rough, Too rude, too boisterous; and it pricks like thorn.

Mercutio. If love be rough with you, be rough with love; Prick love for pricking, and you beat love down.-- Give me a case to put my visage in: [Putting on a mask.] A visard for a visard! what care I What curious eye doth quote deformities? Here are the beetle-brows shall blush for me.

Benvolio. Come, knock and enter; and no sooner in But every man betake him to his legs.

Romeo. A torch for me: let wantons, light of heart,
Tickle the senseless rushes with their heels; For I am
proverb'd with a grandsire phrase,-- I'll be a candle-
holder and look on,-- The game was ne'er so fair, and I
am done.

Mercutio. Tut, dun's the mouse, the constable's own
word: If thou art dun, we'll draw thee from the mire Of
this--sir-reverence--love, wherein thou stick'st Up to the
ears.--Come, we burn daylight, ho.

Romeo. Nay, that's not so.

Mercutio. I mean, sir, in delay We waste our lights
in vain, like lamps by day. Take our good meaning, for
our judgment sits Five times in that ere once in our five
wits.

Romeo. And we mean well, in going to this mask;
But 'tis no wit to go.

Mercutio. Why, may one ask?

Romeo. I dreamt a dream to-night.

Mercutio. And so did I.

Romeo. Well, what was yours?

Mercutio. That dreamers often lie.

Romeo. In bed asleep, while they do dream things true.

Mercutio. O, then, I see Queen Mab hath been with you. She is the fairies' midwife; and she comes In shape no bigger than an agate-stone On the fore-finger of an alderman, Drawn with a team of little atomies Athwart men's noses as they lie asleep: Her waggon-spokes made of long spinners' legs; The cover, of the wings of grasshoppers; The traces, of the smallest spider's web; The collars, of the moonshine's watery beams; Her whip, of cricket's bone; the lash, of film; Her waggoner, a small grey-coated gnat, Not half so big as a round little worm Prick'd from the lazy finger of a maid: Her chariot is an empty hazel-nut, Made by the joiner squirrel or old grub, Time out o' mind the fairies' coachmakers. And in this state she gallops night by night Through lovers' brains, and then they dream of love; O'er courtiers' knees, that dream on court'sies straight; O'er lawyers' fingers, who straight dream on fees; O'er ladies' lips, who straight on kisses dream,-- Which oft the angry Mab with blisters plagues, Because their breaths with sweetmeats tainted are: Sometime she gallops o'er a courtier's nose, And then dreams he of smelling out a suit; And sometime comes she with a tithe-pig's tail, Tickling a parson's nose as 'a lies asleep, Then dreams he of another benefice: Sometime she driveth o'er a soldier's neck, And then dreams he of cutting foreign throats, Of breaches, ambuscadoes, Spanish blades, Of healths five fathom deep; and then anon Drums in his ear, at which he starts and wakes; And, being thus frighted, swears a prayer or two, And sleeps again. This is that very Mab That plats the manes of horses in the night; And bakes the elf-locks in foul sluttish hairs, Which, once untangled, much misfortune bodes: This is the hag, when maids lie on their backs,

That presses them, and learns them first to bear, Making them women of good carriage: This is she,--

Romeo. Peace, peace, Mercutio, peace, Thou talk'st of nothing.

Mercutio. True, I talk of dreams, Which are the children of an idle brain, Begot of nothing but vain fantasy; Which is as thin of substance as the air, And more inconstant than the wind, who wooes Even now the frozen bosom of the north, And, being anger'd, puffs away from thence, Turning his face to the dew-dropping south.

Benvolio. This wind you talk of blows us from ourselves: Supper is done, and we shall come too late.

Romeo. I fear, too early: for my mind misgives Some consequence, yet hanging in the stars, Shall bitterly begin his fearful date With this night's revels; and expire the term Of a despised life, clos'd in my breast, By some vile forfeit of untimely death: But He that hath the steerage of my course Direct my sail!--On,

lusty gentlemen!

Benvolio. Strike, drum.

[Exeunt.]

Scene V. A Hall In Capulet's House.

[Musicians waiting. Enter Servants.]

1 Servant. Where's Potpan, that he helps not to take away? he shift a trencher! he scrape a trencher!

2 Servant. When good manners shall lie all in one or two men's hands, and they unwash'd too, 'tis a foul thing.

1 Servant. Away with the join-stools, remove the court-cupboard, look to the plate:--good thou, save me a piece of marchpane; and as thou loves me, let the porter let in Susan Grindstone and Nell.-- Antony! and Potpan!

2 Servant. Ay, boy, ready.

1 Servant. You are looked for and called for, asked for and sought for in the great chamber.

2 Servant. We cannot be here and there too.-- Cheerly, boys; be brisk awhile, and the longer liver take all.

[They retire behind.]

[Enter Capulet, &c. with the Guests the Maskers.]

Capulet. Welcome, gentlemen! ladies that have their toes Unplagu'd with corns will have a bout with you.-- Ah ha, my mistresses! which of you all Will now deny to dance? she that makes dainty, she, I'll swear hath corns; am I come near you now? Welcome, gentlemen! I have seen the day That I have worn a visard; and could tell A whispering tale in a fair lady's ear, Such as would please;--'tis gone, 'tis gone, 'tis gone: You are welcome, gentlemen!--Come, musicians, play. A hall--a hall! give room! and foot it, girls.-- [Music plays, and they dance.] More light, you knaves; and turn the tables up, And quench the fire, the room is grown too hot.-- Ah, sirrah, this unlook'd-for sport comes well. Nay, sit, nay, sit, good cousin Capulet; For you and I are past our dancing days; How long is't now since last yourself and I Were in a mask?

2 Capulet. By'r Lady, thirty years.

Capulet. What, man! 'tis not so much, 'tis not so much: 'Tis since the nuptial of Lucentio, Come Pentecost as quickly as it will, Some five-and-twenty years; and then we mask'd.

2 Capulet. 'Tis more, 'tis more: his son is elder, sir; His son is thirty.

Capulet. Will you tell me that? His son was but a ward two years ago.

Romeo. What lady is that, which doth enrich the hand Of yonder knight?

Servant. I know not, sir.

Romeo. O, she doth teach the torches to burn bright! It seems she hangs upon the cheek of night Like a rich jewel in an Ethiop's ear; Beauty too rich for use, for earth too dear! So shows a snowy dove trooping with crows As yonder lady o'er her fellows shows. The measure done, I'll watch her place of stand And, touching hers, make blessed my rude hand. Did my heart love till now? forswear it, sight! For I ne'er saw true beauty till this night.

Tybalt. This, by his voice, should be a Montague.-- Fetch me my rapier, boy:--what, dares the slave Come hither, cover'd with an antic face, To fleer and scorn at our solemnity? Now, by the stock and honour of my kin, To strike him dead I hold it not a sin.

Capulet. Why, how now, kinsman! wherefore storm you so?

Tybalt. Uncle, this is a Montague, our foe; A villain, that is hither come in spite, To scorn at our solemnity this night.

Capulet. Young Romeo, is it?

Tybalt. 'Tis he, that villain, Romeo.

Capulet. Content thee, gentle coz, let him alone, He bears him like a portly gentleman; And, to say truth, Verona brags of him To be a virtuous and well-govern'd youth: I would not for the wealth of all the town Here in my house do him disparagement: Therefore be patient, take no note of him,-- It is my will; the which if thou

respect, Show a fair presence and put off these frowns,

An ill-beseeming semblance for a feast.

Tybalt. It fits, when such a villain is a guest: I'll not

endure him.

Capulet. He shall be endur'd: What, goodman boy!--I

say he shall;--go to; Am I the master here, or you? go

to. You'll not endure him!--God shall mend my soul,

You'll make a mutiny among my guests! You will set

cock-a-hoop! you'll be the man!

Tybalt. Why, uncle, 'tis a shame.

Capulet. Go to, go to! You are a saucy boy. Is't so,

indeed?-- This trick may chance to scathe you,--I know

what: You must contrary me! marry, 'tis time.-- Well

said, my hearts!--You are a princox; go: Be quiet, or--

More light, more light!--For shame! I'll make you quiet.

What!--cheerly, my hearts.

Tybalt. Patience perforce with wilful choler meeting

Makes my flesh tremble in their different greeting. I

will withdraw: but this intrusion shall, Now seeming sweet, convert to bitter gall.

[Exit.]

Romeo. [To Juliet.] If I profane with my unworthiest hand This holy shrine, the gentle fine is this,-- My lips, two blushing pilgrims, ready stand To smooth that rough touch with a tender kiss.

Juliet. Good pilgrim, you do wrong your hand too much, Which mannerly devotion shows in this; For saints have hands that pilgrims' hands do touch, And palm to palm is holy palmers' kiss.

Romeo. Have not saints lips, and holy palmers too?

Juliet. Ay, pilgrim, lips that they must use in prayer.

Romeo. O, then, dear saint, let lips do what hands do; They pray, grant thou, lest faith turn to despair.

Juliet. Saints do not move, though grant for prayers' sake.

Romeo. Then move not while my prayer's effect I take. Thus from my lips, by thine my sin is purg'd. [Kissing her.]

Juliet. Then have my lips the sin that they have took.

Romeo. Sin from my lips? O trespass sweetly urg'd! Give me my sin again.

Juliet. You kiss by the book.

Nurse. Madam, your mother craves a word with you.

Romeo. What is her mother?

Nurse. Marry, bachelor, Her mother is the lady of the house. And a good lady, and a wise and virtuous: I nurs'd her daughter that you talk'd withal; I tell you, he that can lay hold of her Shall have the chinks.

Romeo. Is she a Capulet? O dear account! my life is my foe's debt.

Benvolio. Away, be gone; the sport is at the best.

Romeo. Ay, so I fear; the more is my unrest.

Capulet. Nay, gentlemen, prepare not to be gone; We have a trifling foolish banquet towards.-- Is it e'en so?

why then, I thank you all; I thank you, honest gentlemen; good-night.-- More torches here!--Come on then, let's to bed. Ah, sirrah [to 2 Capulet], by my fay, it waxes late; I'll to my rest.

[Exeunt all but Juliet and Nurse.]

Juliet. Come hither, nurse. What is yond gentleman?

Nurse. The son and heir of old Tiberio.

Juliet. What's he that now is going out of door?

Nurse. Marry, that, I think, be young Petruchio.

Juliet. What's he that follows there, that would not dance?

Nurse. I know not.

Juliet. Go ask his name: if he be married, My grave is like to be my wedding-bed.

Nurse. His name is Romeo, and a Montague; The only son of your great enemy.

Juliet. My only love sprung from my only hate! Too early seen unknown, and known too late! Prodigious birth of love it is to me, That I must love a loathed enemy.

Nurse. What's this? What's this?

Juliet. A rhyme I learn'd even now Of one I danc'd withal.

[One calls within, 'Juliet.']

Nurse. Anon, anon! Come, let's away; the strangers all are gone.

[Exeunt.]

[Enter Chorus.]

Chorus. Now old desire doth in his deathbed lie, And young affection gapes to be his heir; That fair for which love groan'd for, and would die, With tender Juliet match'd, is now not fair. Now Romeo is belov'd, and loves again, Alike bewitched by the charm of looks; But to his foe suppos'd he must complain, And she steal love's sweet bait from **fearful** hooks: Being held a foe, he may not have access To breathe such vows as lovers us'd to swear; And she as much in love, her means much less To meet her new beloved anywhere: But passion lends them power, time means, to meet, Tempering extremities with extreme sweet.

[Exit.]

Act II.

Scene I. An Open Place Adjoining Capulet's Garden.

[Enter Romeo.]

Romeo. Can I go forward when my heart is here? Turn back, dull earth, and find thy centre out.

[He climbs the wall and leaps down within it.]

[Enter Benvolio and Mercutio.]

Benvolio. Romeo! my cousin Romeo!

Mercutio. He is wise; And, on my life, hath stol'n him home to bed.

Benvolio. He ran this way, and leap'd this orchard wall: Call, good Mercutio.

Mercutio. Nay, I'll conjure too.-- Romeo! humours! madman! passion! lover! Appear thou in the likeness of a sigh: Speak but one rhyme, and I am satisfied; Cry but 'Ah me!' pronounce but Love and dove; Speak to my gossip Venus one fair word, One nickname for her purblind son and heir, Young auburn Cupid, he that shot so trim When King Cophetua lov'd the beggar-maid!-- He heareth not, he stirreth not, he moveth not; The ape is dead, and I must conjure him.-- I conjure thee by Rosaline's bright eyes, By her high forehead and her scarlet lip, By her fine foot, straight leg, and quivering thigh, And the demesnes that there adjacent lie, That in thy likeness thou appear to us!

Benvolio. An if he hear thee, thou wilt anger him.

Mercutio. This cannot anger him: 'twould anger him To raise a spirit in his mistress' circle, Of some strange nature, letting it there stand Till she had laid it, and conjur'd it down; That were some spite: my invocation Is fair and honest, and, in his mistress' name, I conjure only but to raise up him.

Benvolio. Come, he hath hid himself among these trees, To be consorted with the humorous night: Blind is his love, and best befits the dark.

Mercutio. If love be blind, love cannot hit the mark. Now will he sit under a medlar tree, And wish his mistress were that kind of fruit As maids call medlars when they laugh alone.-- Romeo, good night.--I'll to my truckle-bed; This field-bed is too cold for me to sleep: Come, shall we go?

Benvolio. Go then; for 'tis in vain To seek him here that means not to be found.

[Exeunt.]

Scene II. Capulet's Garden.

[Enter Romeo.]

Romeo. He jests at scars that never felt a wound.--
[Juliet appears above at a window.] But soft! what light
through yonder window breaks? It is the east, and Juliet
is the sun!-- Arise, fair sun, and kill the envious moon,
Who is already sick and pale with grief, That thou her
maid art far more fair than she: Be not her maid, since
she is envious; Her vestal livery is but sick and green,
And none but fools do wear it; cast it off.-- It is my
lady; O, it is my love! O, that she knew she were!-- She
speaks, yet she says nothing: what of that? Her eye
discourses, I will answer it.-- I am too bold, 'tis not to
me she speaks: Two of the fairest stars in all the
heaven, Having some business, do entreat her eyes To
twinkle in their spheres till they return. What if her eyes
were there, they in her head? The brightness of her
cheek would shame those stars, As daylight doth a
lamp; her eyes in heaven Would through the airy region

stream so bright That birds would sing and think it were not night.-- See how she leans her cheek upon her hand! O that I were a glove upon that hand, That I might touch that cheek!

Juliet. Ah me!

Romeo. She speaks:-- O, speak again, bright angel! for thou art As glorious to this night, being o'er my head, As is a winged messenger of heaven Unto the white-upturned wondering eyes Of mortals that fall back to gaze on him When he bestrides the lazy-pacing clouds And sails upon the bosom of the air.

Juliet. O Romeo, Romeo! wherefore art thou Romeo? Deny thy father and refuse thy name; Or, if thou wilt not, be but sworn my love, And I'll no longer be a Capulet.

Romeo. [Aside.] Shall I hear more, or shall I speak at this?

Juliet. 'Tis but thy name that is my enemy;-- Thou art thyself, though not a Montague. What's Montague? It is nor hand, nor foot, Nor arm, nor face, nor any other part Belonging to a man. O, be some other name! What's in a name? that which we call a rose By any other name would smell as sweet; So Romeo would, were he not Romeo call'd, Retain that dear perfection which he owes Without that title:--Romeo, doff thy name; And for that name, which is no part of thee, Take all myself.

Romeo. I take thee at thy word: Call me but love, and I'll be new baptiz'd; Henceforth I never will be Romeo.

Juliet. What man art thou that, thus bescreen'd in night, So stumblest on my counsel?

Romeo. By a name I know not how to tell thee who I am: My name, dear saint, is hateful to myself, Because it is an enemy to thee. Had I it written, I would tear the word.

Juliet. My ears have yet not drunk a hundred words Of that tongue's utterance, yet I know the sound; Art thou not Romeo, and a Montague?

Romeo. Neither, fair saint, if either thee dislike.

Juliet. How cam'st thou hither, tell me, and wherefore? The orchard walls are high and hard to climb; And the place death, considering who thou art, If any of my kinsmen find thee here.

Romeo. With love's light wings did I o'erperch these walls; For stony limits cannot hold love out: And what love can do, that dares love attempt; Therefore thy kinsmen are no let to me.

Juliet. If they do see thee, they will murder thee.

Romeo. Alack, there lies more peril in thine eye Than twenty of their swords: look thou but sweet, And I am proof against their enmity.

Juliet. I would not for the world they saw thee here.

Romeo. I have night's cloak to hide me from their sight; And, but thou love me, let them find me here. My life were better ended by their hate Than death prorogued, wanting of thy love.

Juliet. By whose direction found'st thou out this place?

Romeo. By love, that first did prompt me to enquire; He lent me counsel, and I lent him eyes. I am no pilot; yet, wert thou as far As that vast shore wash'd with the furthest sea, I would adventure for such merchandise.

Juliet. Thou knowest the mask of night is on my face; Else would a maiden blush bepaint my cheek For that which thou hast heard me speak to-night. Fain would I dwell on form,fain, fain deny What I have spoke; but farewell compliment! Dost thou love me, I know thou wilt say Ay; And I will take thy word: yet, if thou swear'st, Thou mayst prove false; at lovers' perjuries, They say Jove laughs. O gentle Romeo, If thou dost love, pronounce it faithfully: Or if thou thinkest I am too quickly won, I'll frown, and be perverse, and say thee nay, So thou wilt woo: but else, not for the world. In truth, fair Montague, I am too fond; And therefore thou mayst think my 'haviour light:

But trust me, gentleman, I'll prove more true Than those that have more cunning to be strange. I should have been more strange, I must confess, But that thou overheard'st, ere I was 'ware, My true-love passion: therefore pardon me; And not impute this yielding to light love, Which the dark night hath so discovered.

Romeo. Lady, by yonder blessed moon I swear, That tips with silver all these fruit-tree tops,--

Juliet. O, swear not by the moon, the inconstant moon, That monthly changes in her circled orb, Lest that thy love prove likewise variable.

Romeo. What shall I swear by?

Juliet. Do not swear at all; Or if thou wilt, swear by thy gracious self, Which is the god of my idolatry, And I'll believe thee.

Romeo. If my heart's dear love,--

Juliet. Well, do not swear: although I joy in thee, I have no joy of this contract to-night; It is too rash, too unadvis'd, too sudden; Too like the lightning, which doth cease to be Ere one can say It lightens. Sweet, good night! This bud of love, by summer's ripening breath, May prove a beauteous flower when next we meet. Good night, good night! as sweet repose and rest Come to thy heart as that within my breast!

Romeo. O, wilt thou leave me so unsatisfied?

Juliet. What satisfaction canst thou have to-night?

Romeo. The exchange of thy love's faithful vow for mine.

Juliet. I gave thee mine before thou didst request it; And yet I would it were to give again.

Romeo. Would'st thou withdraw it? for what purpose, love?

Juliet. But to be frank and give it thee again. And yet I wish but for the thing I have; My bounty is as boundless as the sea, My love as deep; the more I give to thee, The more I have, for both are infinite. I hear some noise within: dear love, adieu!-- [Nurse calls

within.] Anon, good nurse!--Sweet Montague, be true.
Stay but a little, I will come again.

[Exit.]

Romeo. O blessed, blessed night! I am afeard, Being
in night, all this is but a dream, Too flattering-sweet to
be substantial.

[Enter Juliet above.]

Juliet. Three words, dear Romeo, and good night
indeed. If that thy bent of love be honourable, Thy
purpose marriage, send me word to-morrow, By one
that I'll procure to come to thee, Where and what time
thou wilt perform the rite; And all my fortunes at thy
foot I'll lay And follow thee, my lord, throughout the
world.

Nurse. [Within.] Madam!

Juliet. I come anon.-- But if thou meanest not well, I
do beseech thee,--

Nurse. [Within.] Madam!

Juliet. By-and-by I come:-- To cease thy suit and leave me to my grief: To-morrow will I send.

Romeo. So thrive my soul,--

Juliet. A thousand times good night!

[Exit.]

Romeo. A thousand times the worse, to want thy light!-- Love goes toward love as schoolboys from their books; But love from love, towards school with heavy looks.

[Retirong slowly.]

[Re-enter Juliet, above.]

Juliet. Hist! Romeo, hist!--O for a falconer's voice To lure this tassel-gentle back again! Bondage is hoarse and may not speak aloud; Else would I tear the cave where Echo lies, And make her airy tongue more hoarse than mine With repetition of my Romeo's name.

Romeo. It is my soul that calls upon my name: How silver-sweet sound lovers' tongues by night, Like softest music to attending ears!

Juliet. Romeo!

Romeo. My dear?

Juliet. At what o'clock to-morrow Shall I send to thee?

Romeo. At the hour of nine.

Juliet. I will not fail: 'tis twenty years till then. I have forgot why I did call thee back.

Romeo. Let me stand here till thou remember it.

Juliet. I shall forget, to have thee still stand there, Remembering how I love thy company.

Romeo. And I'll still stay, to have thee still forget, Forgetting any other home but this.

Juliet. 'Tis almost morning; I would have thee gone: And yet no farther than a wanton's bird; That lets it hop a little from her hand, Like a poor prisoner in his twisted gyves, And with a silk thread plucks it back again, So loving-jealous of his liberty.

Romeo. I would I were thy bird.

Juliet. Sweet, so would I: Yet I should kill thee with much cherishing. Good night, good night! parting is such sweet sorrow That I shall say good night till it be morrow.

[Exit.]

Romeo. Sleep dwell upon thine eyes, peace in thy breast!-- Would I were sleep and peace, so sweet to rest! Hence will I to my ghostly father's cell, His help to crave and my dear hap to tell.

[Exit.]

Scene III. *Friar Lawrence's Cell.*

[Enter Friar Lawrence with a basket.]

Friar. The grey-ey'd morn smiles on the frowning night, Chequering the eastern clouds with streaks of light; And flecked darkness like a drunkard reels From forth day's path and Titan's fiery wheels: Non, ere the sun advance his burning eye, The day to cheer and night's dank dew to dry, I must up-fill this osier cage of ours With baleful weeds and precious-juiced flowers. The earth, that's nature's mother, is her tomb; What is her burying gave, that is her womb: And from her womb children of divers kind We sucking on her natural bosom find; Many for many virtues excellent, None but for some, and yet all different. O, mickle is the powerful grace that lies In plants, herbs, stones, and their true qualities: For naught so vile that on the earth doth live But to the earth some special good doth give; Nor aught so good but, strain'd from that fair use, Revolts from true birth, stumbling on abuse: Virtue itself turns vice, being misapplied; And vice sometimes by action dignified. Within the infant rind of this small flower Poison hath residence, and medicine power: For this, being smelt, with that part cheers each part; Being tasted, slays all senses with the heart. Two such opposed kings encamp them still In man as well as herbs,--grace and rude will; And where the worser is predominant, Full soon the canker death eats up that plant.

[Enter Romeo.]

Romeo. Good morrow, father!

Friar. Benedicite! What early tongue so sweet saluteth me?-- Young son, it argues a distemper'd head So soon to bid good morrow to thy bed: Care keeps his watch in every old man's eye, And where care lodges sleep will never lie; But where unbruised youth with unstuff'd brain Doth couch his limbs, there golden sleep doth reign: Therefore thy earliness doth me assure Thou art uprous'd with some distemperature; Or if not so, then here I hit it right,-- Our Romeo hath not been in bed to-night.

Romeo. That last is true; the sweeter rest was mine.

Friar. God pardon sin! wast thou with Rosaline?

Romeo. With Rosaline, my ghostly father? no; I have forgot that name, and that name's woe.

Friar. That's my good son: but where hast thou been then?

Romeo. I'll tell thee ere thou ask it me again. I have been feasting with mine enemy; Where, on a sudden, one hath wounded me That's by me wounded. Both our remedies Within thy help and holy physic lies; I bear no hatred, blessed man; for, lo, My intercession likewise steads my foe.

Friar. Be plain, good son, and homely in thy drift; Riddling confession finds but riddling shrift.

Romeo. Then plainly know my heart's dear love is set On the fair daughter of rich Capulet: As mine on hers, so hers is set on mine; And all combin'd, save what thou must combine By holy marriage: when, and where, and how We met, we woo'd, and made exchange of vow, I'll tell thee as we pass; but this I pray, That thou consent to marry us to-day.

Friar. Holy Saint Francis! what a change is here! Is Rosaline, that thou didst love so dear, So soon forsaken? young men's love, then, lies Not truly in their hearts, but in their eyes. Jesu Maria, what a deal of brine Hath wash'd thy sallow cheeks for Rosaline! How much salt water thrown away in waste, To season love, that of it doth not taste! The sun not yet thy sighs from heaven clears, Thy old groans ring yet in mine ancient ears; Lo, here upon thy cheek the stain doth sit Of an old tear that is not wash'd off yet: If e'er thou wast thyself, and these woes thine, Thou and these woes were all for Rosaline; And art thou chang'd? Pronounce this sentence then,-- Women may fall, when there's no strength in men.

Romeo. Thou chidd'st me oft for loving Rosaline.

Friar. For doting, not for loving, pupil mine.

Romeo. And bad'st me bury love.

Friar. Not in a grave To lay one in, another out to have.

Romeo. I pray thee chide not: she whom I love now Doth grace for grace and love for love allow; The other did not so.

Friar. O, she knew well Thy love did read by rote, that could not spell. But come, young waverer, come go with me, In one respect I'll thy assistant be; For this alliance may so happy prove, To turn your households' rancour to pure love.

Romeo. O, let us hence; I stand on sudden haste.

Friar. Wisely, and slow; they stumble that run fast.

[Exeunt.]

Scene IV. A Street.

[Enter Benvolio and Mercutio.]

Mercutio. Where the devil should this Romeo be?-- Came he not home to-night?

Benvolio. Not to his father's; I spoke with his man.

Mercutio. Ah, that same pale hard-hearted wench, that Rosaline, Torments him so that he will sure run mad.

Benvolio. Tybalt, the kinsman to old Capulet, Hath sent a letter to his father's house.

Mercutio. A challenge, on my life.

Benvolio. Romeo will answer it.

Mercutio. Any man that can write may answer a letter.

Benvolio. Nay, he will answer the letter's master, how he dares, being dared.

Mercutio. Alas, poor Romeo, he is already dead! stabbed with a white wench's black eye; shot through the ear with a love song; the very pin of his heart cleft with the blind bow-boy's butt-shaft: and is he a man to encounter Tybalt?

Benvolio. Why, what is Tybalt?

Mercutio. More than prince of cats, I can tell you. O, he's the courageous captain of compliments. He fights as you sing prick-song--keeps time, distance, and proportion; rests me his minim rest, one, two, and the third in your bosom: the very butcher of a silk button, a duellist, a duellist; a gentleman of the very first house,-- of the first and second cause: ah, the immortal passado! the punto reverso! the hay.--

Benvolio. The what?

Mercutio. The pox of such antic, lisping, affecting fantasticoes; these new tuners of accents!--'By Jesu, a very good blade!--a very tall man!--a very good whore!'--Why, is not this a lamentable thing, grandsire, that we should be thus afflicted with these strange flies, these fashion-mongers, these pardonnez-moi's, who stand so much on the new form that they cannot sit at ease on the old bench? O, their bons, their bons!

Benvolio. Here comes Romeo, here comes Romeo!

Mercutio. Without his roe, like a dried herring.--O flesh, flesh, how art thou fishified!--Now is he for the numbers that Petrarch flowed in: Laura, to his lady, was but a kitchen wench,--marry, she had a better love to be-rhyme her; Dido, a dowdy; Cleopatra, a gypsy; Helen and Hero, hildings and harlots; Thisbe, a gray eye or so, but not to the purpose,-

[Enter Romeo.]

Signior Romeo, bon jour! there's a French salutation to your French slop. You gave us the counterfeit fairly last night.

Romeo. Good morrow to you both. What counterfeit did I give you?

Mercutio. The slip, sir, the slip; can you not conceive?

Romeo. Pardon, good Mercutio, my business was great; and in such a case as mine a man may strain courtesy.

Mercutio. That's as much as to say, such a case as yours constrains a man to bow in the hams.

Romeo. Meaning, to court'sy.

Mercutio. Thou hast most kindly hit it.

Romeo. A most courteous exposition.

Mercutio. Nay, I am the very pink of courtesy.

Romeo. Pink for flower.

Mercutio. Right.

Romeo. Why, then is my pump well-flowered.

Mercutio. Well said: follow me this jest now till thou hast worn out thy pump;that, when the single sole of it is worn, the jest may remain, after the wearing, sole singular.

Romeo. O single-soled jest, solely singular for the singleness!

Mercutio. Come between us, good Benvolio; my wits faint.

Romeo. Swits and spurs, swits and spurs; or I'll cry a match.

Mercutio. Nay, if thy wits run the wild-goose chase, I have done; for thou hast more of the wild-goose in one of thy wits than, I am sure, I have in my whole five: was I with you there for the goose?

Romeo. Thou wast never with me for anything when thou wast not there for the goose.

Mercutio. I will bite thee by the ear for that jest.

Romeo. Nay, good goose, bite not.

Mercutio. Thy wit is a very bitter sweeting; it is a most sharp sauce.

Romeo. And is it not, then, well served in to a sweet goose?

Mercutio. O, here's a wit of cheveril, that stretches from an inch narrow to an ell broad!

Romeo. I stretch it out for that word broad: which added to the goose, proves thee far and wide a broad goose.

Mercutio. Why, is not this better now than groaning for love? now art thou sociable, now art thou Romeo; not art thou what thou art, by art as well as by nature: for this drivelling love is like a great natural, that runs lolling up and down to hide his bauble in a hole.

Benvolio. Stop there, stop there.

Mercutio. Thou desirest me to stop in my tale against the hair.

Benvolio. Thou wouldst else have made thy tale large.

Mercutio. O, thou art deceived; I would have made it short: for I was come to the whole depth of my tale; and meant indeed to occupy the argument no longer.

Romeo. Here's goodly gear!

[Enter Nurse and Peter.]

Mercutio. A sail, a sail, a sail!

Benvolio. Two, two; a shirt and a smock.

Nurse. Peter!

Peter. Anon.

Nurse. My fan, Peter.

Mercutio. Good Peter, to hide her face; for her fan's the fairer face.

Nurse. God ye good morrow, gentlemen.

Mercutio. God ye good-den, fair gentlewoman.

Nurse. Is it good-den?

Mercutio. 'Tis no less, I tell ye; for the bawdy hand of the dial is now upon the prick of noon.

Nurse. Out upon you! what a man are you!

Romeo. One, gentlewoman, that God hath made for himself to mar.

Nurse. By my troth, it is well said;--for himself to mar, quoth 'a?--Gentlemen, can any of you tell me where I may find the young Romeo?

Romeo. I can tell you: but young Romeo will be older when you have found him than he was when you sought him: I am the youngest of that name, for fault of a worse.

Nurse. You say well.

Mercutio. Yea, is the worst well? very well took, i' faith; wisely, wisely.

Nurse. If you be he, sir, I desire some confidence with you.

Benvolio. She will indite him to some supper.

Mercutio. A bawd, a bawd, a bawd! So ho!

Romeo. What hast thou found?

Mercutio. No hare, sir; unless a hare, sir, in a lenten pie, that is something stale and hoar ere it be spent. [Sings.] An old hare hoar, And an old hare hoar, Is very good meat in Lent; But a hare that is hoar Is too much for a score When it hoars ere it be spent.

Romeo, will you come to your father's? we'll to dinner thither.

Romeo. I will follow you.

Mercutio. Farewell, ancient lady; farewell,-- [singing] lady, lady, lady.

[Exeunt Mercutio, and Benvolio.]

Nurse. Marry, farewell!--I pray you, sir, what saucy merchant was this that was so full of his ropery?

Romeo. A gentleman, nurse, that loves to hear himself talk; and will speak more in a minute than he will stand to in a month.

Nurse. An 'a speak anything against me, I'll take him down, an'a were lustier than he is, and twenty such Jacks; and if I cannot, I'll find those that shall. Scurvy knave! I am none of his flirt-gills; I am none of his skains-mates.--And thou must stand by too, and suffer every knave to use me at his pleasure!

Peter. I saw no man use you at his pleasure; if I had, my weapon should quickly have been out, I warrant you: I dare draw as soon as another man, if I see occasion in a good quarrel, and the law on my side.

Nurse. Now, afore God, I am so vexed that every part about me quivers. Scurvy knave!--Pray you, sir, a word: and, as I told you, my young lady bid me enquire you out; what she bade me say I will keep to myself: but first let me tell ye, if ye should lead her into a fool's paradise, as they say, it were a very gross kind of behaviour, as they say: for the gentlewoman is young; and, therefore, if you should deal double with her, truly it were an ill thing to be offered to any gentlewoman, and very weak dealing.

Romeo. Nurse, commend me to thy lady and mistress. I protest unto thee,--

Nurse. Good heart, and i' faith I will tell her as much: Lord, Lord, she will be a joyful woman.

Romeo. What wilt thou tell her, nurse? thou dost not mark me.

Nurse. I will tell her, sir,--that you do protest: which, as I take it, is a gentlemanlike offer.

Romeo. Bid her devise some means to come to shrift This afternoon; And there she shall at Friar Lawrence' cell Be shriv'd and married. Here is for thy pains.

Nurse. No, truly, sir; not a penny.

Romeo. Go to; I say you shall.

Nurse. This afternoon, sir? well, she shall be there.

Romeo. And stay, good nurse, behind the abbey-wall: Within this hour my man shall be with thee, And bring thee cords made like a tackled stair; Which to the high top-gallant of my joy Must be my convoy in the secret night. Farewell; be trusty, and I'll quit thy pains: Farewell; commend me to thy mistress.

Nurse. Now God in heaven bless thee!--Hark you, sir.

Romeo. What say'st thou, my dear nurse?

Nurse. Is your man secret? Did you ne'er hear say, Two may keep counsel, putting one away?

Romeo. I warrant thee, my man's as true as steel.

Nurse. Well, sir; my mistress is the sweetest lady.-- Lord, Lord! when 'twas a little prating thing,--O, there's a nobleman in town, one Paris, that would fain lay knife aboard; but she, good soul, had as lief see a toad, a very toad, as see him. I anger her sometimes, and tell her that Paris is the properer man; but I'll warrant you, when I say so, she looks as pale as any clout in the versal world. Doth not rosemary and Romeo begin both with a letter?

Romeo. Ay, nurse; what of that? both with an R.

Nurse. Ah, mocker! that's the dog's name. R is for the dog: no; I know it begins with some other letter:-- and she hath the prettiest sententious of it, of you and rosemary, that it would do you good to hear it.

Romeo. Commend me to thy lady.

Nurse. Ay, a thousand times. [Exit Romeo.]--Peter!

Peter. Anon?

Nurse. Peter, take my fan, and go before.

[Exeunt.]

101

Scene V. Capulet's Garden.

[Enter Juliet.]

Juliet. The clock struck nine when I did send the nurse; In half an hour she promis'd to return. Perchance she cannot meet him: that's not so.-- O, she is lame! love's heralds should be thoughts, Which ten times faster glide than the sun's beams, Driving back shadows over lowering hills: Therefore do nimble-pinion'd doves draw love, And therefore hath the wind-swift Cupid wings. Now is the sun upon the highmost hill Of this day's journey; and from nine till twelve Is three long hours,--yet she is not come. Had she affections and warm youthful blood, She'd be as swift in motion as a ball; My words would bandy her to my sweet love, And his to me: But old folks, many feign as they were dead; Unwieldy, slow, heavy and pale as lead.-- O God, she comes! [Enter Nurse and Peter]. O honey nurse, what news? Hast thou met with him? Send thy man away.

Nurse. Peter, stay at the gate.

[Exit Peter.]

Juliet. Now, good sweet nurse,--O Lord, why look'st thou sad? Though news be sad, yet tell them merrily; If good, thou sham'st the music of sweet news By playing it to me with so sour a face.

Nurse. I am aweary, give me leave awhile;-- Fie, how my bones ache! what a jaunt have I had!

Juliet. I would thou hadst my bones, and I thy news: Nay, come, I pray thee speak;--good, good nurse, speak.

Nurse. Jesu, what haste? can you not stay awhile? Do you not see that I am out of breath?

Juliet. How art thou out of breath, when thou hast breath To say to me that thou art out of breath? The excuse that thou dost make in this delay Is longer than the tale thou dost excuse. Is thy news good or bad? answer to that; Say either, and I'll stay the circumstance: Let me be satisfied, is't good or bad?

Nurse. Well, you have made a simple choice; you know not how to choose a man: Romeo! no, not he; rhough his face be better than any man's, yet his leg excels all men's; and for a hand and a foot, and a body,--though they be not to be talked on, yet they are past compare: he is not the flower of courtesy,--but I'll warrant him as gentle as a lamb.--Go thy ways, wench; serve God.- -What, have you dined at home?

Juliet. No, no: but all this did I know before. What says he of our marriage? what of that?

Nurse. Lord, how my head aches! what a head have I! It beats as it would fall in twenty pieces. My back o' t' other side,--O, my back, my back!-- Beshrew your heart for sending me about To catch my death with jauncing up and down!

Juliet. I' faith, I am sorry that thou art not well. Sweet, sweet, sweet nurse, tell me, what says my love?

Nurse. Your love says, like an honest gentleman,
And a courteous, and a kind, and a handsome; And, I
warrant, a virtuous,--Where is your mother?

Juliet. Where is my mother?--why, she is within;
Where should she be? How oddly thou repliest! 'Your
love says, like an honest gentleman,-- 'Where is your
mother?'

Nurse. O God's lady dear! Are you so hot?
marry,come up, I trow; Is this the poultice for my
aching bones? Henceforward,do your messages
yourself.

Juliet. Here's such a coil!--come, what says Romeo?

Nurse. Have you got leave to go to shrift to-day?

Juliet. I have.

Nurse. Then hie you hence to Friar Lawrence' cell;
There stays a husband to make you a wife: Now comes
the wanton blood up in your cheeks, They'll be in
scarlet straight at any news. Hie you to church; I must
another way, To fetch a ladder, by the which your love

Must climb a bird's nest soon when it is dark: I am the drudge, and toil in your delight; But you shall bear the burden soon at night. Go; I'll to dinner; hie you to the cell.

Juliet. Hie to high fortune!--honest nurse, farewell.

[Exeunt.]

Scene VI. Friar Lawrence's Cell.

[Enter Friar Lawrence and Romeo.]

Friar. So smile the heavens upon this holy act That after-hours with sorrow chide us not!

Romeo. Amen, amen! but come what sorrow can, It cannot countervail the exchange of joy That one short minute gives me in her sight: Do thou but close our hands with holy words, Then love-devouring death do what he dare,-- It is enough I may but call her mine.

Friar. These violent delights have violent ends, And in their triumph die; like fire and powder, Which, as they kiss, consume: the sweetest honey Is loathsome in his own deliciousness, And in the taste confounds the appetite: Therefore love moderately: long love doth so; Too swift arrives as tardy as too slow. Here comes the lady:--O, so light a foot Will ne'er wear out the everlasting flint: A lover may bestride the gossamer That idles in the wanton summer air And yet not fall; so light is vanity.

[Enter Juliet.]

Juliet. Good-even to my ghostly confessor.

Friar. Romeo shall thank thee, daughter, for us both.

Juliet. As much to him, else is his thanks too much.

Romeo. Ah, Juliet, if the measure of thy joy Be heap'd like mine, and that thy skill be more To blazon it, then sweeten with thy breath This neighbour air, and let rich music's tongue Unfold the imagin'd happiness that both Receive in either by this dear encounter.

Juliet. Conceit, more rich in matter than in words, Brags of his substance, not of ornament: They are but beggars that can count their worth; But my true love is grown to such excess, I cannot sum up sum of half my wealth.

Friar. Come, come with me, and we will make short work; For, by your leaves, you shall not stay alone Till holy church incorporate two in one.

[Exeunt.]

Act III.

Scene I. A Public Place.

[Enter Mercutio, Benvolio, Page, and Servants.]

Benvolio. I pray thee, good Mercutio, let's retire: The day is hot, the Capulets abroad, And, if we meet, we shall not scape a brawl; For now, these hot days, is the mad blood stirring.

Mercutio. Thou art like one of these fellows that, when he enters the confines of a tavern, claps me his sword upon the table, and says 'God send me no need of thee!' and by the operation of the second cup draws him on the drawer, when indeed there is no need.

Benvolio. Am I like such a fellow?

Mercutio. Come, come, thou art as hot a Jack in thy mood as any in Italy; and as soon moved to be moody, and as soon moody to be moved.

Benvolio. And what to?

Mercutio. Nay, an there were two such, we should have none shortly, for one would kill the other. Thou! why, thou wilt quarrel with a man that hath a hair more or a hair less in his beard than thou hast. Thou wilt quarrel with a man for cracking nuts, having no other reason but because thou hast hazel eyes;--what eye but such an eye would spy out such a quarrel? Thy head is as full of quarrels as an egg is full of meat; and yet thy head hath been beaten as addle as an egg for quarrelling. Thou hast quarrelled with a man for coughing in the street, because he hath wakened thy dog that hath lain asleep in the sun. Didst thou not fall out with a tailor for wearing his new doublet before Easter? with another for tying his new shoes with an old riband? and yet thou wilt tutor me from quarrelling!

Benvolio. An I were so apt to quarrel as thou art, any man should buy the fee simple of my life for an hour and a quarter.

Mercutio. The fee simple! O simple!

Benvolio. By my head, here come the Capulets.

Mercutio. By my heel, I care not.

[Enter Tybalt and others.]

Tybalt. Follow me close, for I will speak to them.--
Gentlemen, good-den: a word with one of you.

Mercutio. And but one word with one of us? Couple it with something; make it a word and a blow.

Tybalt. You shall find me apt enough to that, sir, an you will give me occasion.

Mercutio. Could you not take some occasion without giving?

Tybalt. Mercutio, thou consortest with Romeo,--

Mercutio. Consort! what, dost thou make us minstrels? An thou make minstrels of us, look to hear nothing but discords: here's my fiddlestick; here's that shall make you dance. Zounds, consort!

Benvolio. We talk here in the public haunt of men: Either withdraw unto some private place, And reason coldly of your grievances, Or else depart; here all eyes gaze on us.

Mercutio. Men's eyes were made to look, and let them gaze; I will not budge for no man's pleasure, I.

Tybalt. Well, peace be with you, sir.--Here comes my man.

[Enter Romeo.]

Mercutio. But I'll be hanged, sir, if he wear your livery: Marry, go before to field, he'll be your follower; Your worship in that sense may call him man.

Tybalt. Romeo, the love I bear thee can afford No better term than this,--Thou art a villain.

Romeo. Tybalt, the reason that I have to love thee Doth much excuse the appertaining rage To such a greeting. Villain am I none; Therefore farewell; I see thou know'st me not.

Tybalt. Boy, this shall not excuse the injuries That thou hast done me; therefore turn and draw.

Romeo. I do protest I never injur'd thee; But love thee better than thou canst devise Till thou shalt know the reason of my love: And so good Capulet,--which name I tender As dearly as mine own,--be satisfied.

Mercutio. O calm, dishonourable, vile submission! Alla stoccata carries it away. [Draws.] Tybalt, you rat-catcher, will you walk?

Tybalt. What wouldst thou have with me?

Mercutio. Good king of cats, nothing but one of your nine lives; that I mean to make bold withal, and, as you shall use me hereafter, dry-beat the rest of the eight. Will you pluck your sword out of his pitcher by the ears? make haste, lest mine be about your ears ere it be out.

Tybalt. I am for you. [Drawing.]

Romeo. Gentle Mercutio, put thy rapier up.

Mercutio. Come, sir, your passado.

[They fight.]

Romeo. Draw, Benvolio; beat down their weapons.-- Gentlemen, for shame! forbear this outrage!-- Tybalt,-- Mercutio,--the prince expressly hath Forbid this bandying in Verona streets.-- Hold, Tybalt!--good Mercutio!-- [Exeunt Tybalt with his Partizans.]

Mercutio. I am hurt;-- A plague o' both your houses!--I am sped.-- Is he gone, and hath nothing?

Benvolio. What, art thou hurt?

Mercutio. Ay, ay, a scratch, a scratch; marry, 'tis enough.-- Where is my page?--go, villain, fetch a surgeon.

Romeo. Courage, man; the hurt cannot be much.

Mercutio. No, 'tis not so deep as a well, nor so wide as a church door; but 'tis enough, 'twill serve: ask for me to-morrow, and you shall find me a grave man. I am peppered, I warrant, for this world.--A plague o' both your houses!--Zounds, a dog, a rat, a mouse, a cat, to scratch a man to death! a braggart, a rogue, a villain, that fights by the book of arithmetic!--Why the devil came you between us? I was hurt under your arm.

Romeo. I thought all for the best.

Mercutio. Help me into some house, Benvolio, Or I shall faint.--A plague o' both your houses! They have made worms' meat of me: I have it, and soundly too.--Your houses!

[Exit Mercutio and Benvolio.]

Romeo. This gentleman, the prince's near ally, My very friend, hath got his mortal hurt In my behalf; my reputation stain'd With Tybalt's slander,--Tybalt, that an hour Hath been my kinsman.--O sweet Juliet, Thy beauty hath made me effeminate And in my temper soften'd valour's steel.

[Re-enter Benvolio.]

Benvolio. O Romeo, Romeo, brave Mercutio's dead! That gallant spirit hath aspir'd the clouds, Which too untimely here did scorn the earth.

Romeo. This day's black fate on more days doth depend; This but begins the woe others must end.

Benvolio. Here comes the furious Tybalt back again.

Romeo. Alive in triumph! and Mercutio slain! Away to heaven respective lenity, And fire-ey'd fury be my conduct now!—

[Re-enter Tybalt.]

Now, Tybalt, take the 'villain' back again That late thou gavest me; for Mercutio's soul Is but a little way above our heads, Staying for thine to keep him company. Either thou or I, or both, must go with him.

Tybalt. Thou, wretched boy, that didst consort him here, Shalt with him hence.

Romeo. This shall determine that.

[They fight; Tybalt falls.]

Benvolio. Romeo, away, be gone! The citizens are up, and Tybalt slain.-- Stand not amaz'd. The prince will doom thee death If thou art taken. Hence, be gone, away!

Romeo. O, I am fortune's fool!

Benvolio. Why dost thou stay?

[Exit Romeo.]

[Enter Citizens, &c.]

1 Citizen. Which way ran he that kill'd Mercutio? Tybalt, that murderer, which way ran he?

Benvolio. There lies that Tybalt.

1 Citizen. Up, sir, go with me; I charge thee in the prince's name obey.

[Enter Prince, attended; Montague, Capulet, their Wives, and others.]

Prince. Where are the vile beginners of this fray?

Benvolio. O noble prince. I can discover all The unlucky manage of this fatal brawl: There lies the man, slain by young Romeo, That slew thy kinsman, brave Mercutio.

Lady Capulet. Tybalt, my cousin! O my brother's child!-- O prince!--O husband!--O, the blood is spill'd Of my dear kinsman!--Prince, as thou art true, For blood of ours shed blood of Montague.-- O cousin, cousin!

Prince. Benvolio, who began this bloody fray?

Benvolio. Tybalt, here slain, whom Romeo's hand did slay; Romeo, that spoke him fair, bid him bethink How nice the quarrel was, and urg'd withal Your high displeasure.--All this,--uttered With gentle breath, calm look, knees humbly bow'd,-- Could not take truce with the unruly spleen Of Tybalt, deaf to peace, but that he tilts With piercing steel at bold Mercutio's breast; Who, all as hot, turns deadly point to point, And, with a martial scorn, with one hand beats Cold death aside, and with the other sends It back to Tybalt, whose dexterity Retorts it: Romeo he cries aloud, 'Hold, friends! friends, part!' and swifter than his tongue, His agile arm beats down their fatal points, And 'twixt them rushes; underneath whose arm An envious thrust from Tybalt hit the life Of stout Mercutio, and then Tybalt fled: But by-and-by comes back to Romeo, Who had but newly entertain'd revenge, And to't they go like lightning; for, ere I Could draw to part them was stout Tybalt slain; And as he fell did Romeo turn and fly. This is the truth, or let Benvolio die.

Lady Capulet. He is a kinsman to the Montague, Affection makes him false, he speaks not true: Some twenty of them fought in this black strife, And all those twenty could but kill one life. I beg for justice, which thou, prince, must give; Romeo slew Tybalt, Romeo must not live.

Prince. Romeo slew him; he slew Mercutio: Who now the price of his dear blood doth owe?

Montague. Not Romeo, prince; he was Mercutio's friend; His fault concludes but what the law should end, The life of Tybalt.

Prince. And for that offence Immediately we do exile him hence: I have an interest in your hate's proceeding, My blood for your rude brawls doth lie a-bleeding; But I'll amerce you with so strong a fine That you shall all repent the loss of mine: I will be deaf to pleading and excuses; Nor tears nor prayers shall purchase out abuses, Therefore use none: let Romeo hence in haste, Else, when he is found, that hour is his last. Bear hence this body, and attend our will: Mercy but murders, pardoning those that kill.

[Exeunt.]

Scene II. A Room In Capulet's House.

[Enter Juliet.]

Juliet. Gallop apace, you fiery-footed steeds, Towards Phoebus' lodging; such a waggoner As Phaeton would whip you to the west And bring in cloudy night immediately.-- Spread thy close curtain, love-performing night! That rude eyes may wink, and Romeo Leap to these arms, untalk'd of and unseen.-- Lovers can see to do their amorous rites By their own beauties: or, if love be blind, It best agrees with night.-- Come, civil night, Thou sober-suited matron, all in black, And learn me how to lose a winning match, Play'd for a pair of stainless maidenhoods: Hood my unmann'd blood, bating in my cheeks, With thy black mantle; till strange love, grown bold, Think true love acted simple modesty. Come, night;--come, Romeo;-- come, thou day in night; For thou wilt lie upon the wings of night Whiter than new snow upon a raven's back.-- Come, gentle night;--come, loving, black-brow'd night, Give me my Romeo; and, when he shall die, Take him and cut him out in little stars, And he will make the face of heaven so fine That all the world will be in love with night, And pay no worship to the garish sun.-- O, I have bought the mansion of a love, But not possess'd it; and, though I am sold, Not yet enjoy'd: so tedious is this day As is the night before some festival To an impatient child that hath new robes, And may not wear them. O, here comes my nurse, And she brings news; and every tongue that speaks But Romeo's name speaks heavenly eloquence.—

[Enter Nurse, with cords.]

Now, nurse, what news? What hast thou there? the cords That Romeo bid thee fetch?

Nurse. Ay, ay, the cords.

[Throws them down.]

Juliet. Ah me! what news? why dost thou wring thy hands?

Nurse. Ah, well-a-day! he's dead, he's dead, he's dead! We are undone, lady, we are undone!-- Alack the day!--he's gone, he's kill'd, he's dead!

Juliet. Can heaven be so envious?

Nurse. Romeo can, Though heaven cannot.--O Romeo, Romeo!-- Who ever would have thought it?-- Romeo!

Juliet. What devil art thou, that dost torment me thus? This torture should be roar'd in dismal hell. Hath Romeo slain himself? say thou but I, And that bare vowel I shall poison more Than the death-darting eye of cockatrice: I am not I if there be such an I; Or those eyes shut that make thee answer I. If he be slain, say I; or if not, no: Brief sounds determine of my weal or woe.

Nurse. I saw the wound, I saw it with mine eyes,-- God save the mark!--here on his manly breast. A piteous corse, a bloody piteous corse; Pale, pale as ashes, all bedaub'd in blood, All in gore-blood;--I swounded at the sight.

Juliet. O, break, my heart!--poor bankrout, break at once! To prison, eyes; ne'er look on liberty! Vile earth, to earth resign; end motion here; And thou and Romeo press one heavy bier!

Nurse. O Tybalt, Tybalt, the best friend I had! O courteous Tybalt! honest gentleman! That ever I should live to see thee dead!

Juliet. What storm is this that blows so contrary? Is Romeo slaughter'd, and is Tybalt dead? My dear-lov'd cousin, and my dearer lord?-- Then, dreadful trumpet, sound the general doom! For who is living, if those two are gone?

Nurse. Tybalt is gone, and Romeo banished; Romeo that kill'd him, he is banished.

Juliet. O God!--did Romeo's hand shed Tybalt's blood?

Nurse. It did, it did; alas the day, it did!

Juliet. O serpent heart, hid with a flowering face! Did ever dragon keep so fair a cave? Beautiful tyrant! fiend angelical! Dove-feather'd raven! wolvish-ravening lamb! Despised substance of divinest show! Just opposite to what thou justly seem'st, A damned saint, an honourable villain!-- O nature, what hadst thou to do in hell When thou didst bower the spirit of a fiend In mortal paradise of such sweet flesh?-- Was ever book containing such vile matter So fairly bound? O, that deceit should dwell In such a gorgeous palace!

Nurse. There's no trust, No faith, no honesty in men; all perjur'd, All forsworn, all naught, all dissemblers.-- Ah, where's my man? Give me some aqua vitae.-- These griefs, these woes, these sorrows make me old. Shame come to Romeo!

Juliet. Blister'd be thy tongue For such a wish! he was not born to shame: Upon his brow shame is asham'd to sit; For 'tis a throne where honour may be crown'd Sole monarch of the universal earth. O, what a beast was I to chide at him!

Nurse. Will you speak well of him that kill'd your cousin?

Juliet. Shall I speak ill of him that is my husband? Ah, poor my lord, what tongue shall smooth thy name, When I, thy three-hours' wife, have mangled it?-- But wherefore, villain, didst thou kill my cousin? That villain cousin would have kill'd my husband: Back, foolish tears, back to your native spring; Your tributary drops belong to woe, Which you, mistaking, offer up to joy. My husband lives, that Tybalt would have slain; And Tybalt's dead, that would have slain my husband: All this is comfort; wherefore weep I, then? Some word there was, worser than Tybalt's death, That murder'd me: I would forget it fain; But O, it presses to my memory Like damned guilty deeds to sinners' minds: 'Tybalt is dead, and Romeo banished.' That 'banished,' that one word 'banished,' Hath slain ten thousand

Tybalts. Tybalt's death Was woe enough, if it had ended there: Or, if sour woe delights in fellowship, And needly will be rank'd with other griefs,-- Why follow'd not, when she said Tybalt's dead, Thy father, or thy mother, nay, or both, Which modern lamentation might have mov'd? But with a rear-ward following Tybalt's death, 'Romeo is banished'--to speak that word Is father, mother, Tybalt, Romeo, Juliet, All slain, all dead: 'Romeo is banished,'-- There is no end, no limit, measure, bound, In that word's death; no words can that woe sound.-- Where is my father and my mother, nurse?

Nurse. Weeping and wailing over Tybalt's corse: Will you go to them? I will bring you thither.

Juliet. Wash they his wounds with tears: mine shall be spent, When theirs are dry, for Romeo's banishment. Take up those cords. Poor ropes, you are beguil'd, Both you and I; for Romeo is exil'd: He made you for a highway to my bed; But I, a maid, die maidenwidowed. Come, cords; come, nurse; I'll to my wedding-bed; And death, not Romeo, take my maidenhead!

Nurse. Hie to your chamber. I'll find Romeo To comfort you: I wot well where he is. Hark ye, your Romeo will be here at night: I'll to him; he is hid at Lawrence' cell.

Juliet. O, find him! give this ring to my true knight, And bid him come to take his last farewell.

[Exeunt.]

Scene III. Friar Lawrence's Cell.

[Enter Friar Lawrence.]

Friar. Romeo, come forth; come forth, thou fearful man. Affliction is enanmour'd of thy parts, And thou art wedded to calamity.

[Enter Romeo.]

Romeo. Father, what news? what is the prince's doom What sorrow craves acquaintance at my hand, That I yet know not?

Friar. Too familiar Is my dear son with such sour company: I bring thee tidings of the prince's doom.

Romeo. What less than doomsday is the prince's doom?

Friar. A gentler judgment vanish'd from his lips,-- Not body's death, but body's banishment.

Romeo. Ha, banishment? be merciful, say death; For exile hath more terror in his look, Much more than death; do not say banishment.

Friar. Hence from Verona art thou banished: Be patient, for the world is broad and wide.

Romeo. There is no world without Verona walls, But purgatory, torture, hell itself. Hence-banished is banish'd from the world, And world's exile is death,-- then banished Is death mis-term'd: calling death banishment, Thou cutt'st my head off with a golden axe, And smil'st upon the stroke that murders me.

Friar. O deadly sin! O rude unthankfulness! Thy fault our law calls death; but the kind prince, Taking thy part, hath brush'd aside the law, And turn'd that black word death to banishment: This is dear mercy, and thou see'st it not.

Romeo. 'Tis torture, and not mercy: heaven is here, Where Juliet lives; and every cat, and dog, And little mouse, every unworthy thing, Live here in heaven, and may look on her; But Romeo may not.--More validity, More honourable state, more courtship lives In carrion flies than Romeo: they may seize On the white wonder of dear Juliet's hand, And steal immortal blessing from her lips; Who, even in pure and vestal modesty, Still blush, as thinking their own kisses sin; But Romeo may not; he is banished,-- This may flies do, when I from this must fly. And sayest thou yet that exile is not death! Hadst thou no poison mix'd, no sharp-ground knife, No sudden mean of death, though ne'er so mean, But banished to kill me; banished? O friar, the damned use that word in hell; Howlings attend it: how hast thou the heart, Being a divine, a ghostly confessor, A sin-absolver, and my friend profess'd, To mangle me with that word banishment?

Friar. Thou fond mad man, hear me speak a little,--

Romeo. O, thou wilt speak again of banishment.

Friar. I'll give thee armour to keep off that word; Adversity's sweet milk, philosophy, To comfort thee, though thou art banished.

Romeo. Yet banished? Hang up philosophy! Unless philosophy can make a Juliet, Displant a town, reverse a prince's doom, It helps not, it prevails not,--talk no more.

Friar. O, then I see that madmen have no ears.

Romeo. How should they, when that wise men have no eyes?

Friar. Let me dispute with thee of thy estate.

Romeo. Thou canst not speak of that thou dost not feel: Wert thou as young as I, Juliet thy love, An hour but married, Tybalt murdered, Doting like me, and like me banished, Then mightst thou speak, then mightst thou tear thy hair, And fall upon the ground, as I do now, Taking the measure of an unmade grave.

[Knocking within.]

Friar. Arise; one knocks. Good Romeo, hide thyself.

Romeo. Not I; unless the breath of heartsick groans, Mist-like infold me from the search of eyes.

[Knocking.]

Friar. Hark, how they knock!--Who's there?--Romeo, arise; Thou wilt be taken.--Stay awhile;--Stand up;

[Knocking.]

Run to my study.--By-and-by!--God's will! What simpleness is this.--I come, I come!

[Knocking.]

Who knocks so hard? whence come you? what's your will?

Nurse. [Within.] Let me come in, and you shall know my errand; I come from Lady Juliet.

Friar. Welcome then.

[Enter Nurse.]

Nurse. O holy friar, O, tell me, holy friar, Where is my lady's lord, where's Romeo?

Friar. There on the ground, with his own tears made drunk.

Nurse. O, he is even in my mistress' case,-- Just in her case!

Friar. O woeful sympathy! Piteous predicament!

Nurse. Even so lies she, Blubbering and weeping, weeping and blubbering.-- Stand up, stand up; stand, an you be a man: For Juliet's sake, for her sake, rise and stand; Why should you fall into so deep an O?

Romeo. Nurse!

Nurse. Ah sir! ah sir!--Well, death's the end of all.

Romeo. Spakest thou of Juliet? how is it with her? Doth not she think me an old murderer, Now I have stain'd the childhood of our joy With blood remov'd but little from her own? Where is she? and how doth she/ and what says My conceal'd lady to our cancell'd love?

Nurse. O, she says nothing, sir, but weeps and weeps; And now falls on her bed; and then starts up, And Tybalt calls; and then on Romeo cries, And then down falls again.

Romeo. As if that name, Shot from the deadly level of a gun, Did murder her; as that name's cursed hand Murder'd her kinsman.--O, tell me, friar, tell me, In what vile part of this anatomy Doth my name lodge? tell me, that I may sack The hateful mansion.

[Drawing his sword.]

Friar. Hold thy desperate hand: Art thou a man? thy form cries out thou art; Thy tears are womanish; thy wild acts denote The unreasonable fury of a beast; Unseemly woman in a seeming man! Or ill-beseeming beast in seeming both! Thou hast amaz'd me: by my holy order, I thought thy disposition better temper'd. Hast thou slain Tybalt? wilt thou slay thyself? And slay thy lady, too, that lives in thee, By doing damned hate upon thyself? Why rail'st thou on thy birth, the heaven, and earth? Since birth and heaven and earth, all three do meet In thee at once; which thou at once wouldst lose. Fie, fie, thou sham'st thy shape, thy love, thy wit; Which, like a usurer, abound'st in all, And usest none in that true use indeed Which should bedeck thy shape, thy love, thy wit: Thy noble shape is but a form of wax, Digressing from the valour of a man; Thy dear love sworn, but hollow perjury, Killing that love which thou hast vow'd to cherish; Thy wit, that ornament to shape and love, Mis-shapen in the conduct of them both, Like powder in a skilless soldier's flask, Is set a-fire by thine own ignorance, And thou dismember'd with thine own defence. What, rouse thee, man! thy Juliet is alive, For whose dear sake thou wast but lately dead; There art thou happy: Tybalt would kill thee, But thou slewest Tybalt; there art thou happy too: The law, that threaten'd death, becomes thy friend, And turns it to exile; there art thou happy: A pack of blessings lights upon thy back; Happiness courts thee in her best array; But, like a misbehav'd and sullen wench, Thou pout'st upon thy fortune and thy love:-- Take heed, take heed, for such die miserable. Go, get thee to thy love, as was decreed, Ascend her chamber, hence and comfort her: But, look, thou stay not till the watch be set, For then thou canst not pass to Mantua; Where thou shalt live till we can find a time To blaze your marriage, reconcile your friends, Beg pardon of the prince, and call thee back With twenty hundred thousand times more joy Than thou went'st forth in lamentation.-- Go before, nurse: commend me to thy lady; And bid her hasten all the house to bed, Which heavy sorrow makes them apt unto. Romeo is coming.

Nurse. O Lord, I could have stay'd here all the night To hear good counsel: O, what learning is!-- My lord, I'll tell my lady you will come.

Romeo. Do so, and bid my sweet prepare to chide.

Nurse. Here, sir, a ring she bid me give you, sir: Hie you, make haste, for it grows very late.

[Exit.]

Romeo. How well my comfort is reviv'd by this!

Friar. Go hence; good night! and here stands all your state: Either be gone before the watch be set, Or by the break of day disguis'd from hence. Sojourn in Mantua; I'll find out your man, And he shall signify from time to time Every good hap to you that chances here: Give me thy hand; 'tis late; farewell; good night.

Romeo. But that a joy past joy calls out on me, It were a grief so brief to part with thee: Farewell.

[Exeunt.]

Scene IV. A Room In Capulet's House.

[Enter Capulet, Lady Capulet, and Paris.]

Capulet. Things have fallen out, sir, so unluckily That we have had no time to move our daughter: Look you, she lov'd her kinsman Tybalt dearly, And so did I; well, we were born to die. 'Tis very late; she'll not come down to-night: I promise you, but for your company, I would have been a-bed an hour ago.

Paris. These times of woe afford no tune to woo.-- Madam, good night: commend me to your daughter.

Lady Capulet. I will, and know her mind early to-morrow; To-night she's mew'd up to her heaviness.

Capulet. Sir Paris, I will make a desperate tender Of my child's love: I think she will be rul'd In all respects by me; nay more, I doubt it not.-- Wife, go you to her ere you go to bed; Acquaint her here of my son Paris' love; And bid her, mark you me, on Wednesday next,-- But, soft! what day is this?

Paris. Monday, my lord.

Capulet. Monday! ha, ha! Well, Wednesday is too soon, Thursday let it be;--a Thursday, tell her, She shall be married to this noble earl.-- Will you be ready? do you like this haste? We'll keep no great ado,--a friend or two; For, hark you, Tybalt being slain so late, It may be thought we held him carelessly, Being our kinsman, if we revel much: Therefore we'll have some half a dozen friends, And there an end. But what say you to Thursday?

Paris. My lord, I would that Thursday were to-morrow.

Capulet. Well, get you gone: o' Thursday be it then.-- Go you to Juliet, ere you go to bed, Prepare her, wife, against this wedding-day.-- Farewell, my lord.--Light to my chamber, ho!-- Afore me, it is so very very late That we may call it early by and by.-- Good night.

[Exeunt.]

Scene V. An Open Gallery to Juliet's Chamber, Overlooking the Garden.

[Enter Romeo and Juliet.]

Juliet. Wilt thou be gone? it is not yet near day: It was the nightingale, and not the lark, That pierc'd the fearful hollow of thine ear; Nightly she sings on yond pomegranate tree: Believe me, love, it was the nightingale.

Romeo. It was the lark, the herald of the morn, No nightingale: look, love, what envious streaks Do lace the severing clouds in yonder east: Night's candles are burnt out, and jocund day Stands tiptoe on the misty mountain tops. I must be gone and live, or stay and die.

Juliet. Yond light is not daylight, I know it, I: It is some meteor that the sun exhales To be to thee this night a torch-bearer And light thee on the way to Mantua: Therefore stay yet, thou need'st not to be gone.

Romeo. Let me be ta'en, let me be put to death; I am content, so thou wilt have it so. I'll say yon gray is not the morning's eye, 'Tis but the pale reflex of Cynthia's brow; Nor that is not the lark whose notes do beat The vaulty heaven so high above our heads: I have more care to stay than will to go.-- Come, death, and welcome! Juliet wills it so.-- How is't, my soul? let's talk,--it is not day.

Juliet. It is, it is!--hie hence, be gone, away! It is the lark that sings so out of tune, Straining harsh discords and unpleasing sharps. Some say the lark makes sweet division; This doth not so, for she divideth us: Some say the lark and loathed toad change eyes; O, now I would they had chang'd voices too! Since arm from arm that voice doth us affray, Hunting thee hence with hunt's-up to the day. O, now be gone; more light and light it grows.

Romeo. More light and light,--more dark and dark our woes!

[Enter Nurse.]

Nurse. Madam!

Juliet. Nurse?

Nurse. Your lady mother is coming to your chamber:
The day is broke; be wary, look about.

[Exit.]

Juliet. Then, window, let day in, and let life out.

Romeo. Farewell, farewell! one kiss, and I'll
descend.

[Descends.]

Juliet. Art thou gone so? my lord, my love, my
friend! I must hear from thee every day i' the hour, For
in a minute there are many days: O, by this count I shall
be much in years Ere I again behold my Romeo!

Romeo. Farewell! I will omit no opportunity That
may convey my greetings, love, to thee.

Juliet. O, think'st thou we shall ever meet again?

Romeo. I doubt it not; and all these woes shall serve For sweet discourses in our time to come.

Juliet. O God! I have an ill-divining soul! Methinks I see thee, now thou art below, As one dead in the bottom of a tomb: Either my eyesight fails, or thou look'st pale.

Romeo. And trust me, love, in my eye so do you: Dry sorrow drinks our blood. Adieu, adieu!

[Exit below.]

Juliet. O fortune, fortune! all men call thee fickle: If thou art fickle, what dost thou with him That is renown'd for faith? Be fickle, fortune; For then, I hope, thou wilt not keep him long But send him back.

Lady Capulet. [Within.] Ho, daughter! are you up?

Juliet. Who is't that calls? is it my lady mother? Is she not down so late, or up so early? What unaccustom'd cause procures her hither?

[Enter Lady Capulet.]

Lady Capulet. Why, how now, Juliet?

Juliet. Madam, I am not well.

Lady Capulet. Evermore weeping for your cousin's death? What, wilt thou wash him from his grave with tears? An if thou couldst, thou couldst not make him live; Therefore have done: some grief shows much of love; But much of grief shows still some want of wit.

Juliet. Yet let me weep for such a feeling loss.

Lady Capulet. So shall you feel the loss, but not the friend Which you weep for.

Juliet. Feeling so the loss, I cannot choose but ever weep the friend.

Lady Capulet. Well, girl, thou weep'st not so much for his death As that the villain lives which slaughter'd him.

Juliet. What villain, madam?

Lady Capulet. That same villain Romeo.

Juliet. Villain and he be many miles asunder.-- God pardon him! I do, with all my heart; And yet no man like he doth grieve my heart.

Lady Capulet. That is because the traitor murderer lives.

Juliet. Ay, madam, from the reach of these my hands. Would none but I might venge my cousin's death!

Lady Capulet. We will have vengeance for it, fear thou not: Then weep no more. I'll send to one in Mantua,-- Where that same banish'd runagate doth live,-- Shall give him such an unaccustom'd dram That he shall soon keep Tybalt company: And then I hope thou wilt be satisfied.

Juliet. Indeed I never shall be satisfied With Romeo till I behold him--dead-- Is my poor heart so for a kinsman vex'd: Madam, if you could find out but a man To bear a poison, I would temper it, That Romeo should, upon receipt thereof, Soon sleep in quiet. O, how my heart abhors To hear him nam'd,--and cannot come to him,-- To wreak the love I bore my cousin Tybalt Upon his body that hath slaughter'd him!

Lady Capulet. Find thou the means, and I'll find such a man. But now I'll tell thee joyful tidings, girl.

Juliet. And joy comes well in such a needy time: What are they, I beseech your ladyship?

Lady Capulet. Well, well, thou hast a careful father, child; One who, to put thee from thy heaviness, Hath sorted out a sudden day of joy That thou expect'st not, nor I look'd not for.

Juliet. Madam, in happy time, what day is that?

Lady Capulet. Marry, my child, early next Thursday morn The gallant, young, and noble gentleman, The County Paris, at St. Peter's Church, Shall happily make thee there a joyful bride.

Juliet. Now by Saint Peter's Church, and Peter too, He shall not make me there a joyful bride. I wonder at this haste; that I must wed Ere he that should be husband comes to woo. I pray you, tell my lord and father, madam, I will not marry yet; and when I do, I swear It shall be Romeo, whom you know I hate, Rather than Paris:--these are news indeed!

Lady Capulet. Here comes your father: tell him so yourself, And see how he will take it at your hands.

[Enter Capulet and Nurse.]

Capulet. When the sun sets, the air doth drizzle dew; But for the sunset of my brother's son It rains downright.-- How now! a conduit, girl? what, still in tears? Evermore showering? In one little body Thou counterfeit'st a bark, a sea, a wind: For still thy eyes, which I may call the sea, Do ebb and flow with tears; the bark thy body is, Sailing in this salt flood; the winds, thy sighs; Who,--raging with thy tears and they with them,-- Without a sudden calm, will overset Thy tempest-tossed body.--How now, wife! Have you deliver'd to her our decree?

Lady Capulet. Ay, sir; but she will none, she gives you thanks. I would the fool were married to her grave!

Capulet. Soft! take me with you, take me with you, wife. How! will she none? doth she not give us thanks? Is she not proud? doth she not count her bles'd, Unworthy as she is, that we have wrought So worthy a gentleman to be her bridegroom?

Juliet. Not proud you have; but thankful that you have: Proud can I never be of what I hate; But thankful even for hate that is meant love.

Capulet. How now, how now, chop-logic! What is this? Proud,--and, I thank you,--and I thank you not;-- And yet not proud:--mistress minion, you, Thank me no thankings, nor proud me no prouds, But fettle your fine joints 'gainst Thursday next To go with Paris to Saint Peter's Church, Or I will drag thee on a hurdle thither. Out, you green-sickness carrion! out, you baggage! You tallow-face!

Lady Capulet. Fie, fie! what, are you mad?

Juliet. Good father, I beseech you on my knees, Hear me with patience but to speak a word.

Capulet. Hang thee, young baggage! disobedient wretch! I tell thee what,--get thee to church o' Thursday, Or never after look me in the face: Speak not, reply not, do not answer me; My fingers itch.--Wife, we scarce thought us bles'd That God had lent us but this only child; But now I see this one is one too much, And that we have a curse in having her: Out on her, hilding!

Nurse. God in heaven bless her!-- You are to blame, my lord, to rate her so.

Capulet. And why, my lady wisdom? hold your tongue, Good prudence; smatter with your gossips, go.

Nurse. I speak no treason.

Capulet. O, God ye good-en!

Nurse. May not one speak?

Capulet. Peace, you mumbling fool! Utter your gravity o'er a gossip's bowl, For here we need it not.

Lady Capulet. You are too hot.

Capulet. God's bread! it makes me mad: Day, night, hour, time, tide, work, play, Alone, in company, still my care hath been To have her match'd, and having now provided A gentleman of noble parentage, Of fair demesnes, youthful, and nobly train'd, Stuff'd, as they say, with honourable parts, Proportion'd as one's heart would wish a man,-- And then to have a wretched puling fool, A whining mammet, in her fortune's tender, To answer, 'I'll not wed,--I cannot love, I am too young,--I pray you pardon me:'-- But, an you will not wed, I'll pardon you: Graze where you will, you shall not house with me: Look to't, think on't, I do not use to jest. Thursday is near; lay hand on heart, advise: An you be mine, I'll give you to my friend; An you be not, hang, beg, starve, die i' the streets, For, by my soul, I'll ne'er acknowledge thee, Nor what is mine shall never do thee good: Trust to't, bethink you, I'll not be forsworn.

[Exit.]

Juliet. Is there no pity sitting in the clouds, That sees into the bottom of my grief? O, sweet my mother, cast me not away! Delay this marriage for a month, a week; Or, if you do not, make the bridal bed In that dim monument where Tybalt lies.

Lady Capulet. Talk not to me, for I'll not speak a word; Do as thou wilt, for I have done with thee.

[Exit.]

Juliet. O God!--O nurse! how shall this be prevented? My husband is on earth, my faith in heaven; How shall that faith return again to earth, Unless that husband send it me from heaven By leaving earth?-- comfort me, counsel me.-- Alack, alack, that heaven should practise stratagems Upon so soft a subject as myself!-- What say'st thou? hast thou not a word of joy? Some comfort, nurse.

Nurse. Faith, here 'tis; Romeo Is banished; and all the world to nothing That he dares ne'er come back to challenge you; Or if he do, it needs must be by stealth. Then, since the case so stands as now it doth, I think it best you married with the county. O, he's a lovely gentleman! Romeo's a dishclout to him; an eagle, madam, Hath not so green, so quick, so fair an eye As Paris hath. Beshrew my very heart, I think you are happy in this second match, For it excels your first: or if it did not, Your first is dead; or 'twere as good he were, As living here, and you no use of him.

Juliet. Speakest thou this from thy heart?

Nurse. And from my soul too; Or else beshrew them both.

Juliet. Amen!

Nurse. What?

Juliet. Well, thou hast comforted me marvellous much. Go in; and tell my lady I am gone, Having displeas'd my father, to Lawrence' cell, To make confession and to be absolv'd.

Nurse. Marry, I will; and this is wisely done.

[Exit.]

Juliet. Ancient damnation! O most wicked fiend! Is it more sin to wish me thus forsworn, Or to dispraise my lord with that same tongue Which she hath prais'd him with above compare So many thousand times?-- Go, counsellor; Thou and my bosom henceforth shall be twain.-- I'll to the friar to know his remedy; If all else fail, myself have power to die.

[Exit.]

Act IV.

Scene I. Friar Lawrence's Cell.

[Enter Friar Lawrence and Paris.]

Friar. On Thursday, sir? the time is very short.

Paris. My father Capulet will have it so; And I am nothing slow to slack his haste.

Friar. You say you do not know the lady's mind: Uneven is the course; I like it not.

Paris. Immoderately she weeps for Tybalt's death, And therefore have I little talk'd of love; For Venus smiles not in a house of tears. Now, sir, her father counts it dangerous That she do give her sorrow so much sway; And, in his wisdom, hastes our marriage, To stop the inundation of her tears; Which, too much minded by herself alone, May be put from her by society: Now do you know the reason of this haste.

Friar. [Aside.] I would I knew not why it should be slow'd.-- Look, sir, here comes the lady toward my cell.

[Enter Juliet.]

Paris. Happily met, my lady and my wife!

Juliet. That may be, sir, when I may be a wife.

Paris. That may be must be, love, on Thursday next.

Juliet. What must be shall be.

Friar. That's a certain text.

Paris. Come you to make confession to this father?

Juliet. To answer that, I should confess to you.

Paris. Do not deny to him that you love me.

Juliet. I will confess to you that I love him.

Paris. So will ye, I am sure, that you love me.

Juliet. If I do so, it will be of more price, Being spoke behind your back than to your face.

Paris. Poor soul, thy face is much abus'd with tears.

Juliet. The tears have got small victory by that; For it was bad enough before their spite.

Paris. Thou wrong'st it more than tears with that report.

Juliet. That is no slander, sir, which is a truth; And what I spake, I spake it to my face.

Paris. Thy face is mine, and thou hast slander'd it.

Juliet. It may be so, for it is not mine own.-- Are you at leisure, holy father, now; Or shall I come to you at evening mass?

Friar. My leisure serves me, pensive daughter, now.-- My lord, we must entreat the time alone.

Paris. God shield I should disturb devotion!-- Juliet, on Thursday early will I rouse you: Till then, adieu; and keep this holy kiss.

[Exit.]

Juliet. O, shut the door! and when thou hast done so, Come weep with me; past hope, past cure, past help!

Friar. Ah, Juliet, I already know thy grief; It strains me past the compass of my wits: I hear thou must, and nothing may prorogue it, On Thursday next be married to this county.

Juliet. Tell me not, friar, that thou hear'st of this, Unless thou tell me how I may prevent it: If, in thy wisdom, thou canst give no help, Do thou but call my resolution wise, And with this knife I'll help it presently. God join'd my heart and Romeo's, thou our hands; And ere this hand, by thee to Romeo's seal'd, Shall be the label to another deed, Or my true heart with treacherous revolt Turn to another, this shall slay them both: Therefore, out of thy long-experienc'd time, Give me some present counsel; or, behold, 'Twixt my extremes and me this bloody knife Shall play the empire; arbitrating that Which the commission of thy years and art Could to no issue of true honour bring. Be not so long to speak; I long to die, If what thou speak'st speak not of remedy.

Friar. Hold, daughter. I do spy a kind of hope, Which craves as desperate an execution As that is desperate which we would prevent. If, rather than to marry County Paris Thou hast the strength of will to slay thyself, Then is it likely thou wilt undertake A thing like death to chide away this shame, That cop'st with death himself to scape from it; And, if thou dar'st, I'll give thee remedy.

Juliet. O, bid me leap, rather than marry Paris, From off the battlements of yonder tower; Or walk in thievish ways; or bid me lurk Where serpents are; chain me with roaring bears; Or shut me nightly in a charnel-house, O'er-cover'd quite with dead men's rattling bones, With reeky shanks and yellow chapless skulls; Or bid me go into a new-made grave, And hide me with a dead man in his shroud; Things that, to hear them told, have made me tremble; And I will do it without fear or doubt, To live an unstain'd wife to my sweet love.

Friar. Hold, then; go home, be merry, give consent To marry Paris: Wednesday is to-morrow; To-morrow night look that thou lie alone, Let not thy nurse lie with thee in thy chamber: Take thou this vial, being then in bed, And this distilled liquor drink thou off: When, presently, through all thy veins shall run A cold and drowsy humour; for no pulse Shall keep his native progress, but surcease: No warmth, no breath, shall testify thou livest; The roses in thy lips and cheeks shall fade To paly ashes; thy eyes' windows fall, Like death, when he shuts up the day of life; Each part, depriv'd of supple government, Shall, stiff and stark and cold, appear like death: And in this borrow'd likeness of shrunk death Thou shalt continue two-and-forty hours, And then awake as from a pleasant sleep. Now, when the bridegroom in the morning comes To rouse thee from thy bed, there art thou dead: Then,--as the manner of our country is,-- In thy best robes, uncover'd, on the bier, Thou shalt be borne to that same ancient vault Where all the kindred of the Capulets lie. In the mean time, against thou shalt awake, Shall Romeo by my letters know our drift; And hither shall he come: and he and I Will watch thy waking, and that very night Shall Romeo bear thee hence to Mantua. And this shall free thee from this present shame, If no inconstant toy nor womanish fear Abate thy valour in the acting it.

Juliet. Give me, give me! O, tell not me of fear!

Friar. Hold; get you gone, be strong and prosperous In this resolve: I'll send a friar with speed To Mantua, with my letters to thy lord.

Juliet. Love give me strength! and strength shall help afford. Farewell, dear father.

[Exeunt.]

Scene II. Hall In Capulet's House.

[Enter Capulet, Lady Capulet, Nurse, and Servants.]

Capulet. So many guests invite as here are writ.--

[Exit first Servant.]

Sirrah, go hire me twenty cunning cooks.

2 Servant. You shall have none ill, sir; for I'll try if they can lick their fingers.

Capulet. How canst thou try them so?

2 Servant. Marry, sir, 'tis an ill cook that cannot lick his own fingers: therefore he that cannot lick his fingers goes not with me.

Capulet. Go, begone.-

[Exit second Servant.]

We shall be much unfurnish'd for this time.-- What, is my daughter gone to Friar Lawrence?

Nurse. Ay, forsooth.

Capulet. Well, be may chance to do some good on her: A peevish self-will'd harlotry it is.

Nurse. See where she comes from shrift with merry look.

[Enter Juliet.]

Capulet. How now, my headstrong! where have you been gadding?

Juliet. Where I have learn'd me to repent the sin Of disobedient opposition To you and your behests; and am enjoin'd By holy Lawrence to fall prostrate here, To beg your pardon:--pardon, I beseech you! Henceforward I am ever rul'd by you.

Capulet. Send for the county; go tell him of this: I'll have this knot knit up to-morrow morning.

Juliet. I met the youthful lord at Lawrence' cell; And gave him what becomed love I might, Not stepping o'er the bounds of modesty.

Capulet. Why, I am glad on't; this is well,--stand up,-- This is as't should be.--Let me see the county; Ay, marry, go, I say, and fetch him hither.-- Now, afore God, this reverend holy friar, All our whole city is much bound to him.

Juliet. Nurse, will you go with me into my closet, To help me sort such needful ornaments As you think fit to furnish me to-morrow?

Lady Capulet. No, not till Thursday; there is time enough.

Capulet. Go, nurse, go with her.--We'll to church to-morrow.

[Exeunt Juliet and Nurse.]

Lady Capulet. We shall be short in our provision: 'Tis now near night.

Capulet. Tush, I will stir about, And all things shall be well, I warrant thee, wife: Go thou to Juliet, help to deck up her; I'll not to bed to-night;--let me alone; I'll play the housewife for this once.--What, ho!-- They are all forth: well, I will walk myself To County Paris, to prepare him up Against to-morrow: my heart is wondrous light Since this same wayward girl is so reclaim'd.

[Exeunt.]

Scene III. Juliet's Chamber.

[Enter Juliet and Nurse.]

Juliet. Ay, those attires are best:--but, gentle nurse, I pray thee, leave me to myself to-night; For I have need of many orisons To move the heavens to smile upon my state, Which, well thou know'st, is cross and full of sin.

[Enter Lady Capulet.]

Lady Capulet. What, are you busy, ho? need you my help?

Juliet. No, madam; we have cull'd such necessaries As are behoveful for our state to-morrow: So please you, let me now be left alone, And let the nurse this night sit up with you; For I am sure you have your hands full all In this so sudden business.

Lady Capulet. Good night: Get thee to bed, and rest; for thou hast need.

[Exeunt Lady Capulet and Nurse.]

Juliet. Farewell!--God knows when we shall meet again. I have a faint cold fear thrills through my veins That almost freezes up the heat of life: I'll call them back again to comfort me;-- Nurse!--What should she do here? My dismal scene I needs must act alone.-- Come, vial.-- What if this mixture do not work at all? Shall I be married, then, to-morrow morning?-- No, No!--this shall forbid it:--lie thou there.—

[Laying down her dagger.]

What if it be a poison, which the friar Subtly hath minister'd to have me dead, Lest in this marriage he should be dishonour'd, Because he married me before to Romeo? I fear it is: and yet methinks it should not, For he hath still been tried a holy man:-- I will not entertain so bad a thought.-- How if, when I am laid into the tomb, I wake before the time that Romeo Come to

167

redeem me? there's a fearful point! Shall I not then be stifled in the vault, To whose foul mouth no healthsome air breathes in, And there die strangled ere my Romeo comes? Or, if I live, is it not very like The horrible conceit of death and night, Together with the terror of the place,-- As in a vault, an ancient receptacle, Where, for this many hundred years, the bones Of all my buried ancestors are pack'd; Where bloody Tybalt, yet but green in earth, Lies festering in his shroud; where, as they say, At some hours in the night spirits resort;-- Alack, alack, is it not like that I, So early waking,--what with loathsome smells, And shrieks like mandrakes torn out of the earth, That living mortals, hearing them, run mad;-- O, if I wake, shall I not be distraught, Environed with all these hideous fears? And madly play with my forefathers' joints? And pluck the mangled Tybalt from his shroud? And, in this rage, with some great kinsman's bone, As with a club, dash out my desperate brains?-- O, look! methinks I see my cousin's ghost

Seeking out Romeo, that did spit his body Upon a rapier's point:--stay, Tybalt, stay!-- Romeo, I come! this do I drink to thee.

[Throws herself on the bed.]

Scene IV. Hall In Capulet's House.

[Enter Lady Capulet and Nurse.]

Lady Capulet. Hold, take these keys and fetch more spices, nurse.

Nurse. They call for dates and quinces in the pastry.

[Enter Capulet.]

Capulet. Come, stir, stir, stir! The second cock hath crow'd, The curfew bell hath rung, 'tis three o'clock:-- Look to the bak'd meats, good Angelica; Spare not for cost.

Nurse. Go, you cot-quean, go, Get you to bed; faith, you'll be sick to-morrow For this night's watching.

Capulet. No, not a whit: what! I have watch'd ere now All night for lesser cause, and ne'er been sick.

Lady Capulet. Ay, you have been a mouse-hunt in your time; But I will watch you from such watching now.

[Exeunt Lady Capulet and Nurse.]

Capulet. A jealous-hood, a jealous-hood!--Now, fellow,

[Enter Servants, with spits, logs and baskets.]

What's there?

1 Servant. Things for the cook, sir; but I know not what.

Capulet. Make haste, make haste. [Exit 1 Servant.] -- Sirrah, fetch drier logs: Call Peter, he will show thee where they are.

2 Servant. I have a head, sir, that will find out logs And never trouble Peter for the matter.

[Exit.]

Capulet. Mass, and well said; a merry whoreson, ha! Thou shalt be logger-head.--Good faith, 'tis day. The county will be here with music straight, For so he said he would:--I hear him near. [Music within.] Nurse!--wife!--what, ho!--what, nurse, I say!

[Re-enter Nurse.]

Go, waken Juliet; go and trim her up; I'll go and chat with Paris:--hie, make haste, Make haste; the bridegroom he is come already: Make haste, I say.

[Exeunt.]

Scene V. Juliet's Chamber; Juliet On the Bed.

[Enter Nurse.]

Nurse. Mistress!--what, mistress!--Juliet!--fast, I warrant her, she:-- Why, lamb!--why, lady!--fie, you slug-abed!-- Why, love, I say!--madam! sweetheart!-- why, bride!-- What, not a word?--you take your pennyworths now; Sleep for a week; for the next night, I warrant, The County Paris hath set up his rest That you shall rest but little.--God forgive me! Marry, and amen, how sound is she asleep! I needs must wake her.- -Madam, madam, madam!-- Ay, let the county take you in your bed; He'll fright you up, i' faith.--Will it not be? What, dress'd! and in your clothes! and down again! I must needs wake you.--lady! lady! lady!-- Alas, alas!-- Help, help! My lady's dead!-- O, well-a-day that ever I was born!-- Some aqua-vitae, ho!--my lord! my lady!

[Enter Lady Capulet.]

Lady Capulet What noise is here?

Nurse. O lamentable day!

Lady Capulet. What is the matter?

Nurse. Look, look! O heavy day!

Lady Capulet. O me, O me!--my child, my only life! Revive, look up, or I will die with thee!-- Help, help!-- call help.

[Enter Capulet.]

Capulet. For shame, bring Juliet forth; her lord is come.

Nurse. She's dead, deceas'd, she's dead; alack the day!

Lady Capulet Alack the day, she's dead, she's dead, she's dead!

Capulet. Ha! let me see her:--out alas! she's cold; Her blood is settled, and her joints are stiff; Life and these lips have long been separated: Death lies on her like an untimely frost Upon the sweetest flower of all the field. Accursed time! unfortunate old man!

Nurse. O lamentable day!

Lady Capulet. O woful time!

Capulet. Death, that hath ta'en her hence to make me wail, Ties up my tongue and will not let me speak.

[Enter Friar Lawrence and Paris, with Musicians.]

Friar. Come, is the bride ready to go to church?

Capulet. Ready to go, but never to return:-- O son, the night before thy wedding day Hath death lain with thy bride:--there she lies, Flower as she was, deflowered by him. Death is my son-in-law, death is my heir; My daughter he hath wedded: I will die. And leave him all; life, living, all is death's.

Paris. Have I thought long to see this morning's face, And doth it give me such a sight as this?

Lady Capulet. Accurs'd, unhappy, wretched, hateful day! Most miserable hour that e'er time saw In lasting labour of his pilgrimage! But one, poor one, one poor and loving child, But one thing to rejoice and solace in, And cruel death hath catch'd it from my sight!

Nurse. O woe! O woeful, woeful, woeful day! Most lamentable day, most woeful day That ever, ever, I did yet behold! O day! O day! O day! O hateful day! Never was seen so black a day as this: O woeful day! O woeful day!

Paris. Beguil'd, divorced, wronged, spited, slain! Most detestable death, by thee beguil'd, By cruel cruel thee quite overthrown!-- O love! O life!--not life, but love in death!

Capulet. Despis'd, distressed, hated, martyr'd, kill'd!-- Uncomfortable time, why cam'st thou now To murder, murder our solemnity?-- O child! O child!--my soul, and not my child!-- Dead art thou, dead!--alack, my child is dead; And with my child my joys are buried!

Friar. Peace, ho, for shame! confusion's cure lives not In these confusions. Heaven and yourself Had part in this fair maid; now heaven hath all, And all the better is it for the maid: Your part in her you could not keep from death; But heaven keeps his part in eternal life. The most you sought was her promotion; For 'twas your heaven she should be advanc'd: And weep ye now, seeing she is advanc'd Above the clouds, as high as heaven itself? O, in this love, you love your child so ill That you run mad, seeing that she is well: She's not well married that lives married long: But she's best married that dies married young. Dry up your tears, and stick your rosemary On this fair corse; and, as the custom is, In all her best array bear her to church; For though fond nature bids us all lament, Yet nature's tears are reason's merriment.

Capulet. All things that we ordained festival Turn from their office to black funeral: Our instruments to melancholy bells; Our wedding cheer to a sad burial feast; Our solemn hymns to sullen dirges change; Our bridal flowers serve for a buried corse, And all things change them to the contrary.

Friar. Sir, go you in,--and, madam, go with him;-- And go, Sir Paris;--every one prepare To follow this fair corse unto her grave: The heavens do lower upon you for some ill; Move them no more by crossing their high will.

[Exeunt Capulet, Lady Capulet, Paris, and Friar.]

1 Musician. Faith, we may put up our pipes and be gone.

Nurse. Honest good fellows, ah, put up, put up; For well you know this is a pitiful case.

[Exit.]

1 Musician. Ay, by my troth, the case may be amended.

[Enter Peter.]

Peter. Musicians, O, musicians, 'Heart's ease,' 'Heart's ease': O, an you will have me live, play 'Heart's ease.'

1 Musician. Why 'Heart's ease'?

Peter. O, musicians, because my heart itself plays 'My heart is full of woe': O, play me some merry dump to comfort me.

1 Musician. Not a dump we: 'tis no time to play now.

Peter. You will not then?

1 Musician. No.

Peter. I will then give it you soundly.

1 Musician. What will you give us?

Peter. No money, on my faith; but the gleek,--I will give you the minstrel.

1 Musician. Then will I give you the serving-creature.

Peter. Then will I lay the serving-creature's dagger on your pate. I will carry no crotchets: I'll re you, I'll fa you: do you note me?

1 Musician. An you re us and fa us, you note us.

2 Musician. Pray you put up your dagger, and put out your wit.

Peter. Then have at you with my wit! I will dry-beat you with an iron wit, and put up my iron dagger.-- Answer me like men:

'When griping grief the heart doth wound, And doleful dumps the mind oppress, Then music with her silver sound'--

why 'silver sound'? why 'music with her silver sound'?-- What say you, Simon Catling?

1 Musician. Marry, sir, because silver hath a sweet sound.

Peter. Pretty!--What say you, Hugh Rebeck?

2 Musician. I say 'silver sound' because musicians sound for silver.

Peter. Pretty too!--What say you, James Soundpost?

3 Musician. Faith, I know not what to say.

Peter. O, I cry you mercy; you are the singer: I will say for you. It is 'music with her silver sound' because musicians have no gold for sounding:--

'Then music with her silver sound With speedy help doth lend redress.'

[Exit.]

1 Musician. What a pestilent knave is this same!

2 Musician. Hang him, Jack!--Come, we'll in here; tarry for the mourners, and stay dinner.

[Exeunt.]

Act V.

Scene I. Mantua. A Street.

[Enter Romeo.]

Romeo. If I may trust the flattering eye of sleep, My dreams presage some joyful news at hand; My bosom's lord sits lightly in his throne; And all this day an unaccustom'd spirit Lifts me above the ground with cheerful thoughts. I dreamt my lady came and found me dead,-- Strange dream, that gives a dead man leave to think!-- And breath'd such life with kisses in my lips, That I reviv'd, and was an emperor. Ah me! how sweet is love itself possess'd, When but love's shadows are so rich in joy!

[Enter Balthasar.]

News from Verona!--How now, Balthasar? Dost thou not bring me letters from the friar? How doth my lady? Is my father well? How fares my Juliet? that I ask again; For nothing can be ill if she be well.

Balthasar. Then she is well, and nothing can be ill: Her body sleeps in Capel's monument, And her immortal part with angels lives. I saw her laid low in her kindred's vault, And presently took post to tell it you: O, pardon me for bringing these ill news, Since you did leave it for my office, sir.

Romeo. Is it even so? then I defy you, stars!-- Thou know'st my lodging: get me ink and paper, And hire post-horses. I will hence to-night.

Balthasar. I do beseech you, sir, have patience: Your looks are pale and wild, and do import Some misadventure.

Romeo. Tush, thou art deceiv'd: Leave me, and do the thing I bid thee do. Hast thou no letters to me from the friar?

Balthasar. No, my good lord.

Romeo. No matter: get thee gone, And hire those horses; I'll be with thee straight.

[Exit Balthasar.]

Well, Juliet, I will lie with thee to-night. Let's see for means;--O mischief, thou art swift To enter in the thoughts of desperate men! I do remember an apothecary,-- And hereabouts he dwells,--which late I noted In tatter'd weeds, with overwhelming brows, Culling of simples; meagre were his looks, Sharp misery had worn him to the bones; And in his needy shop a tortoise hung, An alligator stuff'd, and other skins Of ill-shaped fishes; and about his shelves A beggarly account of empty boxes, Green earthen pots, bladders, and musty seeds, Remnants of packthread, and old cakes of roses, Were thinly scatter'd, to make up a show. Noting this penury, to myself I said, An if a man did need a poison now, Whose sale is present death in Mantua, Here lives a caitiff wretch would sell it him. O, this same thought did but forerun my need; And this same needy man must sell it me. As I remember, this should be the house: Being holiday, the beggar's shop is shut.-- What, ho! apothecary!

[Enter Apothecary.]

Apothecary. Who calls so loud?

Romeo. Come hither, man.--I see that thou art poor; Hold, there is forty ducats: let me have A dram of poison; such soon-speeding gear As will disperse itself through all the veins That the life-weary taker mall fall dead; And that the trunk may be discharg'd of breath As violently as hasty powder fir'd Doth hurry from the fatal cannon's womb.

Apothecary. Such mortal drugs I have; but Mantua's law Is death to any he that utters them.

Romeo. Art thou so bare and full of wretchedness And fear'st to die? famine is in thy cheeks, Need and oppression starveth in thine eyes, Contempt and beggary hangs upon thy back, The world is not thy friend, nor the world's law: The world affords no law to make thee rich; Then be not poor, but break it and take this.

Apothecary. My poverty, but not my will consents.

Romeo. I pay thy poverty, and not thy will.

Apothecary. Put this in any liquid thing you will, And drink it off; and, if you had the strength Of twenty men, it would despatch you straight.

Romeo. There is thy gold; worse poison to men's souls, Doing more murders in this loathsome world Than these poor compounds that thou mayst not sell: I sell thee poison; thou hast sold me none. Farewell: buy food and get thyself in flesh.-- Come, cordial and not poison, go with me To Juliet's grave; for there must I use thee.

[Exeunt.]

Scene II. Friar Lawrence's Cell.

[Enter Friar John.]

Friar John. Holy Franciscan friar! brother, ho!

[Enter Friar Lawrence.]

Friar Lawrence. This same should be the voice of Friar John. Welcome from Mantua: what says Romeo? Or, if his mind be writ, give me his letter.

Friar John. Going to find a barefoot brother out, One of our order, to associate me, Here in this city visiting the sick, And finding him, the searchers of the town, Suspecting that we both were in a house Where the infectious pestilence did reign, Seal'd up the doors, and would not let us forth; So that my speed to Mantua there was stay'd.

Friar Lawrence. Who bare my letter, then, to Romeo?

Friar John. I could not send it,--here it is again,-- Nor get a messenger to bring it thee, So fearful were they of infection.

Friar Lawrence. Unhappy fortune! by my brotherhood, The letter was not nice, but full of charge Of dear import; and the neglecting it May do much danger. Friar John, go hence; Get me an iron crow and bring it straight Unto my cell.

Friar John. Brother, I'll go and bring it thee.

[Exit.]

Friar Lawrence. Now must I to the monument alone; Within this three hours will fair Juliet wake: She will beshrew me much that Romeo Hath had no notice of these accidents; But I will write again to Mantua, And keep her at my cell till Romeo come;-- Poor living corse, clos'd in a dead man's tomb!

Scene III. A Churchyard; In It a Monument

Belonging to the Capulets.

[Enter Paris, and his Page bearing flowers and a torch.]

Paris. Give me thy torch, boy: hence, and stand aloof;-- Yet put it out, for I would not be seen. Under yond yew tree lay thee all along, Holding thine ear close to the hollow ground; So shall no foot upon the churchyard tread,-- Being loose, unfirm, with digging up of graves,-- But thou shalt hear it: whistle then to me, As signal that thou hear'st something approach. Give me those flowers. Do as I bid thee, go.

Page. [Aside.] I am almost afraid to stand alone Here in the churchyard; yet I will adventure.

[Retires.]

Paris. Sweet flower, with flowers thy bridal bed I strew: O woe! thy canopy is dust and stones! Which with sweet water nightly I will dew; Or, wanting that, with tears distill'd by moans: The obsequies that I for thee will keep, Nightly shall be to strew thy grave and weep.

[The Page whistles.]

The boy gives warning something doth approach. What cursed foot wanders this way to-night, To cross my obsequies and true love's rite? What, with a torch! muffle me, night, awhile.

[Retires.]

[Enter Romeo and Balthasar with a torch, mattock, &c.]

Romeo. Give me that mattock and the wrenching iron. Hold, take this letter; early in the morning See thou deliver it to my lord and father. Give me the light;

upon thy life I charge thee, Whate'er thou hear'st or seest, stand all aloof And do not interrupt me in my course. Why I descend into this bed of death Is partly to behold my lady's face, But chiefly to take thence from her dead finger A precious ring,--a ring that I must use In dear employment: therefore hence, be gone:-- But if thou, jealous, dost return to pry In what I further shall intend to do, By heaven, I will tear thee joint by joint, And strew this hungry churchyard with thy limbs: The time and my intents are savage-wild; More fierce and more inexorable far Than empty tigers or the roaring sea.

Balthasar. I will be gone, sir, and not trouble you.

Romeo. So shalt thou show me friendship.--Take thou that: Live, and be prosperous: and farewell, good fellow.

Balthasar. For all this same, I'll hide me hereabout: His looks I fear, and his intents I doubt.

[Retires.]

Romeo. Thou detestable maw, thou womb of death,
Gorg'd with the dearest morsel of the earth, Thus I
enforce thy rotten jaws to open,

[Breaking open the door of the monument.]

And, in despite, I'll cram thee with more food!

Paris. This is that banish'd haughty Montague That
murder'd my love's cousin,--with which grief, It is
supposed, the fair creature died,-- And here is come to
do some villanous shame To the dead bodies: I will
apprehend him.—

[Advances.]

Stop thy unhallow'd toil, vile Montague! Can
vengeance be pursu'd further than death? Condemned
villain, I do apprehend thee; Obey, and go with me; for
thou must die.

Romeo. I must indeed; and therefore came I hither.--
Good gentle youth, tempt not a desperate man; Fly
hence and leave me:--think upon these gone; Let them
affright thee.--I beseech thee, youth, Put not another sin
upon my head By urging me to fury: O, be gone! By
heaven, I love thee better than myself; For I come hither
arm'd against myself: Stay not, be gone;--live, and
hereafter say, A madman's mercy bid thee run away.

Paris. I do defy thy conjurations, And apprehend
thee for a felon here.

Romeo. Wilt thou provoke me? then have at thee,
boy!

[They fight.]

Page. O lord, they fight! I will go call the watch.
[Exit.]

Paris. O, I am slain! [Falls.] If thou be merciful,
Open the tomb, lay me with Juliet.

[Dies.]

Romeo. In faith, I will.--Let me peruse this face:--
Mercutio's kinsman, noble County Paris!-- What said
my man, when my betossed soul Did not attend him as
we rode? I think He told me Paris should have married
Juliet: Said he not so? or did I dream it so? Or am I
mad, hearing him talk of Juliet, To think it was so?--O,
give me thy hand, One writ with me in sour
misfortune's book! I'll bury thee in a triumphant grave;-
- A grave? O, no, a lanthorn, slaught'red youth, For here
lies Juliet, and her beauty makes This vault a feasting
presence full of light. Death, lie thou there, by a dead
man interr'd.

[Laying Paris in the monument.]

How oft when men are at the point of death Have they been merry! which their keepers call A lightning before death: O, how may I Call this a lightning?--O my love! my wife! Death, that hath suck'd the honey of thy breath, Hath had no power yet upon thy beauty: Thou art not conquer'd; beauty's ensign yet Is crimson in thy lips and in thy cheeks, And death's pale flag is not advanced there.-- Tybalt, liest thou there in thy bloody sheet? O, what more favour can I do to thee Than with that hand that cut thy youth in twain To sunder his that was thine enemy? Forgive me, cousin!--Ah, dear Juliet, Why art thou yet so fair? Shall I believe That unsubstantial death is amorous; And that the lean abhorred monster keeps Thee here in dark to be his paramour? For fear of that I still will stay with thee, And never from this palace of dim night Depart again: here, here will I remain With worms that are thy chambermaids: O, here Will I set up my everlasting rest; And shake the yoke of inauspicious stars From this world-wearied flesh.--Eyes, look your last! Arms, take your last embrace! and, lips, O you The doors of breath, seal with a righteous kiss A dateless bargain to engrossing death!-- Come, bitter conduct, come, unsavoury guide! Thou desperate pilot, now at once run on The dashing rocks thy sea-sick weary bark! Here's to my love! [Drinks.]--O true apothecary! Thy drugs are quick.--Thus with a kiss I die.

[Dies.]

[Enter, at the other end of the Churchyard, Friar Lawrence, with a lantern, crow, and spade.]

Friar. Saint Francis be my speed! how oft to-night Have my old feet stumbled at graves!--Who's there? Who is it that consorts, so late, the dead?

Balthasar. Here's one, a friend, and one that knows you well.

Friar. Bliss be upon you! Tell me, good my friend, What torch is yond that vainly lends his light To grubs and eyeless skulls? as I discern, It burneth in the Capels' monument.

Balthasar. It doth so, holy sir; and there's my master, One that you love.

Friar. Who is it?

Balthasar. Romeo.

Friar. How long hath he been there?

Balthasar. Full half an hour.

Friar. Go with me to the vault.

Balthasar. I dare not, sir; My master knows not but I am gone hence; And fearfully did menace me with death If I did stay to look on his intents.

Friar. Stay then; I'll go alone:--fear comes upon me; O, much I fear some ill unlucky thing.

Balthasar. As I did sleep under this yew tree here, I dreamt my master and another fought, And that my master slew him.

Friar. Romeo! [Advances.] Alack, alack! what blood is this which stains The stony entrance of this sepulchre?-- What mean these masterless and gory swords To lie discolour'd by this place of peace?

[Enters the monument.]

Romeo! O, pale!--Who else? what, Paris too? And steep'd in blood?--Ah, what an unkind hour Is guilty of this lamentable chance!--The lady stirs.

[Juliet wakes and stirs.]

Juliet. O comfortable friar! where is my lord?-- I do remember well where I should be, And there I am:-- where is my Romeo?

[Noise within.]

Friar. I hear some noise.--Lady, come from that nest Of death, contagion, and unnatural sleep: A greater power than we can contradict Hath thwarted our intents:--come, come away! Thy husband in thy bosom there lies dead; And Paris too:--come, I'll dispose of thee Among a sisterhood of holy nuns: Stay not to question, for the watch is coming. Come, go, good Juliet [noise within],--I dare no longer stay.

Juliet. Go, get thee hence, for I will not away.--

[Exit Friar Lawrence.]

What's here? a cup, clos'd in my true love's hand? Poison, I see, hath been his timeless end:-- O churl! drink all, and left no friendly drop To help me after?--I will kiss thy lips; Haply some poison yet doth hang on them, To make me die with a restorative.

[Kisses him.]

Thy lips are warm!

1 Watch. [Within.] Lead, boy:--which way?

Juliet. Yea, noise?--Then I'll be brief.--O happy dagger!

[Snatching Romeo's dagger.]

This is thy sheath [stabs herself]; there rest, and let me die.

[Falls on Romeo's body and dies.]

[Enter Watch, with the Page of Paris.]

Page. This is the place; there, where the torch doth burn.

1 Watch. The ground is bloody; search about the churchyard: Go, some of you, whoe'er you find attach.

[Exeunt some of the Watch.]

Pitiful sight! here lies the county slain;-- And Juliet bleeding; warm, and newly dead, Who here hath lain this two days buried.-- Go, tell the prince;--run to the Capulets,-- Raise up the Montagues,--some others search:--

[Exeunt others of the Watch.]

We see the ground whereon these woes do lie; But the true ground of all these piteous woes We cannot without circumstance descry.

[Re-enter some of the Watch with Balthasar.]

2 Watch. Here's Romeo's man; we found him in the churchyard.

1 Watch. Hold him in safety till the prince come hither.

[Re-enter others of the Watch with Friar Lawrence.]

3 Watch. Here is a friar, that trembles, sighs, and weeps: We took this mattock and this spade from him As he was coming from this churchyard side.

1 Watch. A great suspicion: stay the friar too.

[Enter the Prince and Attendants.]

Prince. What misadventure is so early up, That calls our person from our morning's rest?

[Enter Capulet, Lady Capulet, and others.]

Capulet. What should it be, that they so shriek abroad?

Lady Capulet. The people in the street cry Romeo, Some Juliet, and some Paris; and all run, With open outcry, toward our monument.

Prince. What fear is this which startles in our ears?

1 Watch. Sovereign, here lies the County Paris slain; And Romeo dead; and Juliet, dead before, Warm and new kill'd.

Prince. Search, seek, and know how this foul murder comes.

1 Watch. Here is a friar, and slaughter'd Romeo's man, With instruments upon them fit to open These dead men's tombs.

Capulet. O heaven!--O wife, look how our daughter bleeds! This dagger hath mista'en,--for, lo, his house Is empty on the back of Montague,-- And it mis-sheathed in my daughter's bosom!

Lady Capulet. O me! this sight of death is as a bell That warns my old age to a sepulchre.

[Enter Montague and others.]

Prince. Come, Montague; for thou art early up, To see thy son and heir more early down.

Montague. Alas, my liege, my wife is dead to-night; Grief of my son's exile hath stopp'd her breath: What further woe conspires against mine age?

Prince. Look, and thou shalt see.

Montague. O thou untaught! what manners is in this, To press before thy father to a grave?

Prince. Seal up the mouth of outrage for a while, Till we can clear these ambiguities, And know their spring, their head, their true descent; And then will I be general of your woes, And lead you even to death: meantime forbear, And let mischance be slave to patience.-- Bring forth the parties of suspicion.

Friar. I am the greatest, able to do least, Yet most suspected, as the time and place Doth make against me, of this direful murder; And here I stand, both to impeach and purge Myself condemned and myself excus'd.

Prince. Then say at once what thou dost know in this.

Friar. I will be brief, for my short date of breath Is not so long as is a tedious tale. Romeo, there dead, was husband to that Juliet; And she, there dead, that Romeo's faithful wife: I married them; and their stol'n marriage day Was Tybalt's doomsday, whose untimely death Banish'd the new-made bridegroom from this city; For whom, and not for Tybalt, Juliet pin'd. You, to remove that siege of grief from her, Betroth'd, and would have married her perforce, To County Paris:-- then comes she to me, And with wild looks, bid me devise some means To rid her from this second marriage, Or in my cell there would she kill herself. Then gave I her, so tutored by my art, A sleeping potion; which so took effect As I intended, for it wrought on her The form of death: meantime I writ to Romeo That he should hither come as this dire night, To help to take her from her borrow'd grave, Being the time the potion's force should cease. But he which bore my letter, Friar John, Was stay'd by accident; and yesternight Return'd my letter back. Then all alone At the prefixed hour of her waking Came I to take her from her kindred's vault; Meaning to keep her closely at my cell Till I conveniently could send to Romeo: But when

I came,--some minute ere the time Of her awaking,--
here untimely lay The noble Paris and true Romeo
dead. She wakes; and I entreated her come forth And
bear this work of heaven with patience: But then a noise
did scare me from the tomb; And she, too desperate,
would not go with me, But, as it seems, did violence on
herself. All this I know; and to the marriage Her nurse
is privy: and if ought in this Miscarried by my fault, let
my old life Be sacrific'd, some hour before his time,
Unto the rigour of severest law.

Prince. We still have known thee for a holy man.--
Where's Romeo's man? what can he say in this?

Balthasar. I brought my master news of Juliet's
death; And then in post he came from Mantua To this
same place, to this same monument. This letter he early
bid me give his father; And threaten'd me with death,
going in the vault, If I departed not, and left him there.

Prince. Give me the letter,--I will look on it.-- Where is the county's page that rais'd the watch?-- Sirrah, what made your master in this place?

Boy. He came with flowers to strew his lady's grave; And bid me stand aloof, and so I did: Anon comes one with light to ope the tomb; And by-and-by my master drew on him; And then I ran away to call the watch.

Prince. This letter doth make good the friar's words, Their course of love, the tidings of her death: And here he writes that he did buy a poison Of a poor 'pothecary, and therewithal Came to this vault to die, and lie with Juliet.-- Where be these enemies?--Capulet,-- Montague,-- See what a scourge is laid upon your hate, That heaven finds means to kill your joys with love! And I, for winking at your discords too, Have lost a brace of kinsmen:--all are punish'd.

Capulet. O brother Montague, give me thy hand: This is my daughter's jointure, for no more Can I demand.

Montague. But I can give thee more: For I will raise her statue in pure gold; That while Verona by that name is known, There shall no figure at such rate be set As that of true and faithful Juliet.

Capulet. As rich shall Romeo's by his lady's lie; Poor sacrifices of our enmity!

Prince. A glooming peace this morning with it brings; The sun for sorrow will not show his head. Go hence, to have more talk of these sad things; Some shall be pardon'd, and some punished; For never was a story of more woe Than this of Juliet and her Romeo.

[Exeunt.]

CPSIA information can be obtained at www.ICGtesting.com
Printed in the USA
LVOW04s1414050914

402645LV00010B/154/P